PHOENIX
BLACKWINGS MC BOOK THREE

BY

TEAGAN BROOKS

Cathy
♡ Teagan Brooks

Dedication

To everyone who believes in true love.

Contents

PART ONE

CHAPTER ONE

Phoenix

21 years ago

It was the first week of summer, and I was at a field party with some of my buddies from the football team. If this one was going to be anything like the last two summers, we would practice every day during the week and find somewhere to party all weekend. Rinse and repeat. I wasn't a huge fan of partying all the time, but this was the first one of the summer, and I was pretty excited.

My best friend, Aaron, grabbed the cooler from the back of my truck, and we made our way over to the other members of our team by the bonfire.

I was enjoying shooting the shit with the guys

when Aaron nudged me with his elbow. "Those two over by Douchey Dave's Camaro have been looking over here every few minutes. Let's go over and talk to them."

I really wasn't interested in picking up a girl, but I was the dutiful friend and played his wingman. "Lead the way."

"Dibs on the brunette."

I rolled my eyes, thinking he didn't need to call dibs because he could have whichever one he wanted. As we neared the girls and my eyes landed on the blonde, I was quick to lay claim to her. She was breathtaking. I quickly scanned her body from the golden blonde hair that fell below her shoulders leading to her ample chest, to her flat stomach and curvy hips, to her bare, tanned legs. As we got closer, her baby blue eyes flicked to me, and her pouty lips curled into a shy smile. "Dibs on the blonde," I muttered.

He slapped me on the back. "That's the spirit, my man."

Aaron sauntered up to the girls and introduced us. "Hello, ladies, I don't believe we've met. I'm Aaron Marshall, and this is Phoenix Black," he said, extending his hand to the brunette with a smile that he'd used to charm the pants off many.

The brunette grasped his hand and returned his smile. "I'm Macy McManis, and this is Annabelle Burnett."

Annabelle shook his hand and turned her eyes to me. "Hi," she said with a shy smile.

"Hi," I repeated and proceeded to stare at her like an idiot.

Aaron cleared his throat. "So, you girls must not be from Croftridge because I would most definitely remember seeing your beautiful faces."

Macy giggled. "I live in Cedar Valley. Annabelle's family just moved to Croftridge last week."

"Where did you move from?" I asked Annabelle.

"A little town not far from Reedy Fork."

"Which one? I have some cousins that live up that way in Devil Springs." When her cheeks turned pink, and she ducked her head, I knew. "You lived in Crapper, didn't you?" I asked softly.

She nodded. "I'm so glad we moved."

She was obviously uncomfortable. Not only did Crapper have a shitty name, but it was also a very poor town. I was afraid she was going to bolt, so I quickly changed the subject. "So, how did you girls meet?" I asked.

Macy started to answer, "Annabelle's mother—"

"—and Macy's mother work together,"

4

Annabelle interrupted. Macy shot her a sideways glance, but didn't say anything else.

"So, you'll be going to Croftridge High in the fall?" I asked.

"Yes, I'll be a senior."

I smiled. "Me, too." She looked down and shuffled her feet. "It must suck having to go to a new school for your senior year," I said, trying to get her to talk to me.

She looked up and shrugged. "This will be my third high school, so it's not really a big deal."

"Oh. So, what brought your family to Croftridge?"

She grimaced. "My grandmother passed away, and my mother inherited her house."

"I'm sorry to hear that."

She shrugged. "Thanks, but it wasn't a huge thing for me. I mean, it sucks that she died, but I never met the woman."

Again, I sensed her discomfort and changed the subject. I started rambling about Croftridge and things to do around the area, which admittedly wasn't much.

"You seem to know a lot about Croftridge. Have you always lived here?"

"No, I was born in California and lived there until my parents died in a car accident when I was 15. My father's parents died before I was born, so I moved to Croftridge to live with my mother's parents."

"You'll love the Blacks. Gram and Pop are two of the nicest people you'll ever meet," Aaron interjected.

When Annabelle's brows furrowed in confusion, I knew what was coming. "How is your last name Black?"

I chuckled. "Caught that, did ya? Oddly enough, my mother and father had the same last name."

She seemed to relax as we continued talking and getting to know each other. Completely enthralled with her, I failed to pay attention to the others around us, or the time. I had never met anyone like her and was fully captivated from the moment we exchanged our first words.

It was hours later when she looked at the time and gasped. "I need to find Macy and get home before I miss my curfew."

She stood and scanned the area for her friend. I stood as well and looked for Aaron, but didn't see him anywhere.

"Shit," Annabelle cursed. "Her car's gone."

"I can take you home," I offered.

"No, I couldn't ask you to do that."

"You didn't ask. I offered. Come on," I said and nudged her with my elbow.

"I don't know..." she said warily.

"I had one beer tonight, and that was hours ago." I held my hands up and met her eyes. "I promise, I just want to make sure you get home safely. My Gram would whoop my ass if she found out I knowingly left a young woman stranded in an unfamiliar place with strangers at night." That was the truth, too. Gram and Pop had taught me to look out for others and offer help when help was needed.

While we walked to my truck, I pulled out my phone and called Aaron. "Where the fuck are you?" I growled into the phone when he answered.

The sounds of heavy breathing and female moaning filled my ears, causing me to sigh. "Never mind, I know where you are."

"You're gonna take her girl home, right?" he asked, clearly not taking a break from his exertions.

"It's a little late to be asking, don't you think?" I snapped.

"Nah, I knew you would take care of her."

"Fuck off, Aaron."

"Trying to," he laughed and ended the call.

I opened the passenger door for Annabelle and gestured for her to get in. "Your friend left with Aaron."

"She's not really my friend."

"Oh? You mentioned your mothers worked together, so I just assumed you two were friends."

"My mother cleans her parents' house. She was sick a few days last week, and I had to fill in for her. While I was there, I met Macy, and she invited me to this party," she said with a shrug.

"I'm glad she did. I enjoyed meeting you," I said softly.

"Yeah, me, too."

I followed the directions Annabelle gave me to her house. When I pulled up to a rundown house on the outskirts of town, I didn't want to let her out of my truck. But, I kept my mouth shut because I didn't want her to feel embarrassed. I didn't care where she came from or how much money her family had, but I did care about her safety.

I tipped my head toward the dark structure. "Are your parents home?"

"My mom should be," she muttered. I felt marginally better knowing she wouldn't be alone.

"You want to go get lunch tomorrow? Maybe I can show you around Croftridge," I blurted.

"Yeah, that sounds nice."

"Okay, doll face. I'll pick you up at 12:00 pm tomorrow."

"Okay."

"Okay."

After a few beats of awkward silence, I cupped the side of her face with my hand and brought my lips to hers. Nothing overly passionate or intense, just a soft, lingering kiss. I wanted her to know I was interested, but I didn't want to scare her off by being too forward.

"Do you want me to walk you to the door?"

"No, my mother will raise hell if she finds out a guy brought me home."

"I'll wait here until you're inside," I said softly.

"Good night, Phoenix."

As I watched her walk into the dark, dilapidated house, I knew, right then and there, she walked into that house carrying my heart in her hands.

CHAPTER TWO

Phoenix

I saw Annabelle every day for the rest of the summer. During the weekdays, I had football practice, and she worked at my Gram's shop when she wasn't helping her mother clean Macy's parents' house, but the evenings and weekends were ours. To me, it didn't matter what we did or who we were with, as long as the two of us were together.

When school started, I picked Annabelle up every morning and drove us to school. In the afternoons, she drove my truck to Gram's shop to work for a few hours while I was at practice. I hated that she worked so much, but she told me she was trying to save as much as she could so she wouldn't have to work much when she went off to college. And I believed her, until a month before the Homecoming football game and dance, when the nominations for Homecoming King and Queen were made.

I wasn't surprised in the least when Annabelle was nominated. Yes, she was new to the school, but she quickly became the sweetheart of our little town. Annabelle, however, was completely caught off guard by the nomination and didn't seem too happy about it.

On the way home from school that day, I finally asked her, "Doll face, what's wrong?"

She remained silent for several minutes before finally giving it to me. "Phoenix, I don't have the money to be a part of the Homecoming festivities. I'll need to buy a new dress, shoes, jewelry, pay to have my hair done. I just can't afford it."

I wanted to offer to buy her dress and everything else she needed, but I knew from past experience she wouldn't like it. So, I tried a different tactic. "You know, Gram is one hell of a bargain shopper. You'd be surprised at some of the deals she's come across. I bet she could help you find a dress for a steal."

Annabelle turned hopeful eyes to me. "You think she can help me find what I need for less than $50?"

I smiled. "I know she can, doll face. I'll talk to her when I get home."

Gram was more than willing to help Annabelle. She, too, wanted to buy her a nice dress, but I explained Annabelle's feelings about having things handed to her. Gram grinned as if she knew something I didn't. "Well, I guess we will have to start shopping tomorrow."

The next afternoon, Annabelle and Gram went shopping and returned home with what looked like a brand new dress, matching shoes, jewelry, and a purse. Annabelle squealed with delight when she pulled the dress from the bag to show me. "We got all of this for $30! Can you believe it, Phoenix? Look, the dress still has the tags on it!"

"It's beautiful," I said, smiling at how happy she was. "A beautiful dress for a beautiful girl."

I knew Gram's friend owned the local thrift shop. I had no doubt Gram bought the dress and accessories in Cedar Valley and dropped it off with her friend to hold for Annabelle and only Annabelle.

Before Annabelle and I left to meet up with Macy and Aaron for dinner and a movie, I hugged Gram and whispered my thanks into her ear.

She winked and shrugged. "I just went shopping." Yeah, twice, I thought.

***

Since Aaron and I had to be at the school early for the Homecoming football game, Annabelle and Macy decided to get ready at Macy's house and ride to the game together. Macy didn't go to school with us, but she was escorting Aaron onto the field when the players were announced. Annabelle, of course, was escorting me.

When I caught sight of her walking onto the field, my breath seized in my chest. She smiled as she neared me and all I could do was stare. I still hadn't moved or made a sound when she reached me. "Phoenix?" she asked worriedly. "Is everything okay?"

At the sound of uncertainty in her voice, my faculties came back online. "You are undoubtedly the most beautiful woman in the world," I breathed.

She blushed and cast her eyes to the ground. "Thank you, Phoenix."

After they announced the team, she went back to the stands with Macy while Aaron and I took to the field. I was the starting quarterback and Aaron was the starting left tackle. Since we were both seniors and it was our last Homecoming game, the coach kept us in the game for the entire first half, which meant I was a stinky, sweaty mess by half-time.

I had less than 20 minutes to get out of my football gear, shower as fast as humanly possible, put on my Homecoming clothes, and get back to the field for the Homecoming court announcements. I pushed through the locker room doors and ran to the field, coming to a stop beside Annabelle.

"I was worried you wouldn't make it in time," she whispered.

"I almost didn't," I whispered back, right as our names sounded over the speaker. We took our place on the field and waited while the other nominees were announced.

I will openly admit I was nervous. For her, not for me. I couldn't care less if I won Homecoming King or not. What I didn't want to happen was for me to win and her not to. I was so lost in my thoughts I didn't realize I had missed something until Annabelle jabbed me with her elbow and whisper-yelled, "Phoenix, go!"

I stepped forward, unsure of what was happening until I saw someone coming at me with an obnoxiously large, fake crown. Fuck me. I won.

I stood in front of the court, facing the packed stands, nervously glancing around and waiting for the next announcement. And draw it out, they did. The microphone was tested, as if it hadn't been working properly the entire night. The announcer took a sip of water. The envelope was dropped. When the girl started to fumble with the envelope like she couldn't get it open, I couldn't take it anymore. I yanked it from her hands, ripped it open, and said into the microphone, "This year's Homecoming Queen is my girl, Annabelle Burnett."

I turned and extended my hand to her. She immediately stepped forward and took it. Once she was crowned, I cupped her cheek and gave her a chaste kiss. Then, against her lips, I whispered the words I had wanted to say for some time, "I love you, Annabelle."

She grinned. "I love you, too, Phoenix."

CHAPTER THREE

Annabelle

After Homecoming, my relationship with Phoenix was different, in a good way. I think hearing the words "I love you" from him was what I needed to stop holding back. I no longer felt the need to hide the true nature of my home life from him. So, when he took me home one night in November and asked if anyone was home because the house was so dark, I answered him honestly.

"It's dark because we don't have any power," I said softly.

"Annabelle—," he started, but I cut him off.

"Phoenix, my parents aren't like your grandparents. My mother is a drunk, and my father is hardly ever home. He only comes home for a day, two at the most, before he takes off again. He doesn't help with the bills, and my mom lost her job with Macy's parents not long after school started. When she didn't show up for work, and I couldn't fill in for her, Macy's parents had no choice but to fire her," I explained.

He rubbed his chin with his thumb and forefinger. "You aren't working for Gram to save money for college, are you?"

"No, I'm not. I'm sorry for lying to you. You come from such a good family, and I was embarrassed by mine."

"Annabelle, I don't give a shit about what kind of parents you have or where you come from. I care about you. I love you, doll face. Now, please let me help you," he pleaded.

"I can't, Phoenix. I just can't," I said, starting to get upset.

"Okay, okay," he relented. "But I can't let you stay in that house without power. It's too cold, baby. Come spend the night in one of Gram's guest rooms, and we'll figure something out tomorrow, okay?"

"Your grandparents won't mind?" I asked.

"No, they won't, as long as you stay in your room, and I stay in mine."

As much as I didn't want to accept any handouts, the thought of a warm and cozy bed was too good to pass up. "Okay. Just for tonight."

"Just for tonight," he agreed and squeezed my hand.

The next morning, I nervously left the guest room and tiptoed down the stairs. I found Phoenix and his grandparents in the kitchen, seemingly waiting for me.

"Good morning," I shakily said to the room.

"Good morning, sweetheart," Gram said. "Did you sleep okay?"

"Yes, ma'am. Thank you for letting me stay," I said uncomfortably.

She smiled. "Have a seat, dear. We were just about to have breakfast."

I took a seat while she brought everything to the table and began handing out food. Phoenix's grandfather cleared his throat and placed his clasped hands on the table. "Annabelle, Phoenix told us a little about your situation at home. I admire you for trying to take on the responsibilities of your parents, and I respect you for not wanting to accept handouts. Those are admirable qualities that are hard to find in most adults and rarely, if ever, found in teenagers. But, sweetheart, you do need some help, or at least a little luck. I grew up in Croftridge, and with the exception of the time I was away at college, I've always lived here, in this very house. As a result, I've accumulated a large number of customer loyalty points with various service providers that I'll never use. I made a few phone calls this morning and was able to use my loyalty points for the utilities at your address. Starting today, you'll have power, water, and heat for the next year, and it didn't cost me or anyone else a penny."

Completely flabbergasted, I stared at the man for a few long beats before I moved to hug him and simultaneously burst into tears. "Thank you, Mr. Black. Thank you so much."

He returned my embrace and patted my back. "You're very welcome, sweetheart. We were happy to help."

When I returned home later that day, the power was on, the heat was working, and we had hot water. I was thrilled. My mother was too drunk to notice.

CHAPTER FOUR

Phoenix

The house smelled like cookies. It always did on Christmas Eve.

Gram was in the kitchen making her traditional Christmas treats with flour everywhere, even streaked across her smiling face.

Her smile fell when she saw me. "Honey, is something wrong?"

I shifted my weight from foot to foot. "No, Gram, nothing's wrong. I just wanted to ask if I could invite Annabelle over for Christmas?"

"Of course, you can. You didn't even need to ask."

"Gram, I'm asking if she can spend the night

in one of the guest rooms. Her parents don't celebrate the holidays and probably won't even be home. I can't stand the thought of her spending Christmas alone in that house."

Gram crossed the kitchen and patted my cheek with her flour covered hand. "No one should ever be alone on Christmas. Go get our girl."

There was no need to tell me twice. I was out the door and across town as fast as I could safely get there.

"Phoenix, what are you doing here?" Annabelle asked when she opened her flimsy front door.

"Go pack a bag, doll face. You're spending Christmas with us."

Her mouth opened and closed. "I can't," she stammered.

"Why not? Are your parents here?"

She shook her head. "No, they're not, but I can't impose on your family's Christmas."

"You're not imposing. Gram told me to come get you. She's always said no one should spend the holidays alone. Grab your stuff and let's go. I'm sure she could use your help making cookies."

I stumbled back a step when Annabelle unexpectedly launched herself into my arms. "Thank you," she whispered against my neck.

I waited in the living room while she gathered her things, taking in the sparse surroundings. I hated that she was forced to live in such deplorable conditions, but there wasn't much I could do about it at the time.

It only took her a few minutes to return with her backpack and a large shopping bag full of wrapped presents. I took the bags from her and asked, "Is that everything?"

She shuffled her feet and looked away from me as her cheeks flushed.

"What is it, doll face?"

She cleared her throat, but wouldn't meet my eyes. "Can I bring my tree?"

Her voice was so quiet I wasn't sure I heard her correctly, but it didn't matter what she said, it wouldn't change my answer. "You can bring whatever you want. Let me put your bags in the truck first and I'll get it for you."

When I returned, she led me to her bedroom. In the corner of her room, she had a small artificial Christmas tree with a few ornaments on it. It couldn't have been more than three feet tall and would easily fit in the back seat of my truck.

"I know it's silly, but this is the only tree I've ever had, and I don't want to spend Christmas without it," she explained, looking embarrassed.

"Baby, it's not silly. Do you have a garbage bag we can slide over it so the ornaments won't get broken if they come off while we're moving it?"

Once the ornaments were secured, we loaded her tree and drove back to my house. Annabelle was unusually quiet during the ride, but she did hold my hand the entire way. I wasn't sure if she was still feeling embarrassed about her tree or if it had something to do with her parents. Either way, I thought it was best to give her time to work through her feelings. I knew she would talk to me about it when she was ready.

When we pulled into the driveway, I told her, "Go on inside. Gram's in the kitchen making goodies. I'll take your things inside and put them in the room you stayed in last time."

"Thanks, Phoenix," she whispered and kissed my cheek before getting out and going inside.

As I carefully carried her tree up the stairs, I vowed then and there to do everything I could to make her Christmas special. I had a feeling it was something her parents had never bothered to do for her.

CHAPTER FIVE

Annabelle

I nervously entered the kitchen to find Phoenix's grandmother flitting around from mixing bowl to mixing bowl. "Hi, Gram," I said softly.

She whirled around with a bright smile on her face. "Annabelle, my dear, want to help me with the Christmas goodies?"

I returned her smile. "I'm not sure how much help I will be. I don't have much experience with baking, but I'm willing to try."

She waved her hand in the air dismissively. "There's nothing to it. I'll show you everything you need to know."

And she did. I spent the next few hours in

the kitchen making everything from basic sugar cookies to some fancy chocolate covered truffle I had never heard of.

"Are you planning on feeding an army with all of this?" I asked. There wasn't an inch of counter space that didn't have a container full of treats covering it by the time we were finished.

Gram laughed. "Sort of. Tomorrow, we're driving up to Devil Springs to see Tommy's brother and his family. He started a motorcycle club there years ago, and I always make treats for the members. Some of them have their own family, but a lot of them don't, and I like to make sure they feel included in the festivities."

I wasn't sure what to say, and Gram must have thought my silence was due to being scared of the motorcycle club. "Don't you worry about a thing, dear. Those men may look rough and tough, but they're all a bunch a big teddy bears. I hope you brought an extra change of clothes with you. We usually spend the night at the clubhouse and drive home the next day."

"I did, but Phoenix only mentioned me spending the night tonight."

Gram chuckled. "What exactly did he say?"

"That I was spending Christmas with you all."

"Exactly. Christmas is a three-day event in

this family. Why don't you see if you can round up Phoenix? I'll have dinner ready in about 45 minutes."

I found Phoenix in his bedroom. When I knocked on his open door, he yanked a blanket over something and quickly stood in front of it. "What are you doing?"

"Trying to wrap your present. Go away."

I laughed. "If you were so worried about it, you should have closed the door."

He scoffed. "Yeah, well, I thought you would still be in the kitchen with Gram. I didn't know it would be this hard to wrap a present."

"You've never wrapped a present before?"

He shook his head. "No, I haven't. Gram wraps Pop's for me, and Pop wraps Gram's. My mom and dad used to do the same before they died."

"Okay, I'll leave you to it. Gram said dinner would be ready in about 45 minutes. I'm going to wash this flour off and change clothes."

After dinner, Gram ushered us into the living room to open presents. "When Phoenix was little, we used to open presents in the morning, but now that he's older, we exchange our gifts on Christmas Eve so we can leave for Devil Springs right after breakfast," she explained and headed for the tree.

Pop started a fire in the fireplace while Gram passed out presents. I was beyond amazed at the pile of gifts in front of me. It was too much. As if reading my mind, Gram said, "I know what you're thinking, dear. Tommy and I have been blessed with more than enough to live out the rest of our days comfortably. It brings me great joy to share our good fortune with others. Merry Christmas, sweetheart."

What could I say to that? Absolutely nothing. So, I smiled and opened the gifts in front of me while I tried not to cry. When I was finished, I had a pile of clothes, shoes, a new backpack, a new purse, some earrings, and a few gift cards.

I looked up when I heard a gasp. Gram was holding my gift to her in her hands. "Tommy, look at this," she said and turned the frame to her husband.

"What is it?" Phoenix asked, climbing out from under his pile of presents to take a look.

"It's the most beautiful picture of an elephant I've ever seen. Oh, Annabelle, where did you find this?" Gram asked.

Before I could answer, Phoenix did. "She didn't find it, Gram. She drew it. See her signature right there in the corner."

Gram turned her wide eyes to me. "You did

this?" At my nod, she hugged the frame to her chest. "It's exquisite. I will forever cherish it."

I felt my eyes begin to tear up at her kind words. Thankfully, Pop broke the emotionally charged moment when he started eagerly digging through his pile of gifts. "Don't just stand there, help me find mine, love!"

I giggled and reached over to pull my gift to him from the pile. He took it from my outstretched hand and ripped the paper open. Beaming from ear to ear, he turned the frame around and proudly showed everyone the pirate schooner I had drawn for him. "I love it," he declared.

I smiled shyly. I didn't have much money, but I wanted to give them something special for Christmas. I knew Gram loved elephants, and Pop had an affinity for pirate ships, so I spent a few weeks working on the drawings for them. I was relieved by their reactions. I, personally, thought the drawings were some of my best work, but I had no idea what they would think.

Phoenix stood and crossed his arms. "And where is mine?"

I felt my cheeks heat. I had one for him as well, but I had planned on giving it to him without an audience. "It's upstairs. I didn't realize we were exchanging our gifts now," I said quietly.

He stepped closer and cupped my cheek. "Relax, doll face. I was only kidding."

"If you want to smack him, we'll pretend like we didn't see it," Pop interjected causing us all to laugh.

By the time we finished opening gifts and cleaning up the mess of wrapping paper and ribbons, it was late, and I was ready to go to sleep. After hugging Gram and Pop and saying good night, I turned to Phoenix to do the same. He pulled me against his chest and whispered in my ear, "Come to my room after they go to bed so we can exchange gifts." Without giving me a chance to respond, he kissed my cheek and said loud enough for Gram and Pop to hear, "Good night, doll face. Merry Christmas!"

I waited in my room until I heard Gram and Pop come upstairs and close their bedroom door. Then, I waited another 15 minutes before I tiptoed down the hall and quietly knocked on Phoenix's door.

He answered the door wearing nothing but a pair of flannel sleep pants that sat low on his hips. I had seen his body before, but never when we were alone with a door that locked and a bed. I briefly wondered if I was drooling before he placed his finger under my chin and tilted

29

my head. "You gotta stop looking at me like that, baby. I'm trying to behave myself," he said huskily.

"Then put a fucking shirt on," I blurted.

He chuckled, but did as I said and pulled a t-shirt on over his head.

I took a seat on the edge of the bed and tried not to tear at the wrapping paper while I waited for him to get my gift. I don't know why I was so nervous. I knew Phoenix wouldn't care if I hadn't gotten him anything, and we had been alone together many times before, so there was no reason for me to feel the need to get to my feet and bolt from the room.

I felt the bed depress beside me followed by Phoenix's warmth at my side. He placed his large palm on my bouncing thigh and asked, "You okay, doll face?"

"Yeah," I croaked and cleared my throat. "Sorry. I'm nervous, and I don't know why."

He cupped my cheek with his other hand and pressed a soft kiss to my lips. "No reason for you to be nervous, baby."

"I know," I whispered against his lips.

He scooted back and grinned. "I'll go first so you can actually enjoy opening your presents." At my nod, he picked up the smaller of the two gifts I had for him. He made a great show of inspecting the gift and shaking it before he finally opened it.

His eyes widened, and he sucked in a breath when he pulled the black leather chain wallet from the box. On the front, it had a phoenix etched into the leather. I wouldn't have been able to get it for him, but Gram gave me an unexpected Christmas bonus at the beginning of the month.

Phoenix continued to stare at the wallet, and I started to get worried. Finally, he met my eyes and smiled. "I love it."

Breathing a sigh of relief, I handed him the other gift, though I was sure he knew what it was.

He took it from me and didn't delay in ripping the paper off. "Annabelle, this is by far your best one yet," he said with a smile as he admired the framed drawing of a phoenix.

"Thank you," I murmured.

He studied the picture for a few more moments before he put it down and handed me a fairly large box. I looked at the box and giggled. "I'm guessing you didn't ask anyone to help you with the wrapping."

"Shut it, doll face, and start opening."

I did as I was told and made quick work of removing the paper and opening the box. Inside I found a plethora of art supplies. And not the kind of art supplies I was used to using. No, these were the top of the line, name brand, ones I'd only dreamed about having kind of art supplies.

With my hand covering my gaping mouth, I looked up to thank him, but he spoke before I was able to formulate words. "You have an amazing talent, doll face. You should have the tools you need to sharpen your skills."

"Thank you," I said softly as one tear slid down my face, which I quickly wiped away.

He handed me another gift in a much smaller box. I took it from him and carefully unwrapped it to find a black velvet box. I froze, unsure of what to do.

"It's not what you think, sweetheart. Open it," Phoenix said softly.

I nodded and slowly opened the box. Beautifully displayed on the black fabric was a necklace with matching earrings, and they were a perfect replication of the tiny Phoenix I drew all over anything I could draw on.

Glancing between the box in my hand and Phoenix, I asked, "How did you do this?"

He shrugged. "Gram isn't the only one with

tricks in this town. Though, if you sue me for violating your copyrights, I may be forced to reveal my sources."

I playfully slapped his chest. "You know I'm not going to do that."

He grabbed my wrist and pulled me against his chest. "I know," he said and fell to his back on the bed, taking me with him. Before I could protest, his hand curved around the back of my head and held me in place while he took my lips in a heated kiss.

"Phoenix, we can't," I weakly protested.

"We're not," he breathed. "Just let me love on you for a few minutes."

It was hard to pull myself out of Phoenix's arms and return to my room, but out of respect for Gram and Pop, we managed to separate ourselves.

As I slid into bed and pulled the covers over me, I couldn't keep the smile off my face. It had been the best Christmas ever, and it wasn't even technically Christmas yet.

CHAPTER SIX

Annabelle

After breakfast, we drove to Devil Springs to spend the day with Phoenix's extended family, at a motorcycle club compound. I didn't know much about motorcycle clubs, but the things I had heard about motorcycle gangs made me incredibly nervous. The closer we got, the antsier I became.

"You okay, doll face?"

"Yeah," I swallowed and nodded. "I'm just a little nervous about meeting the rest of your family."

Phoenix snorted. "You're going to lie to me on Christmas?"

"What?" I asked, trying to sound surprised.

"You're lying to me. What is it? Are you worried about the bikers?"

I focused on my clasped hands in my lap. "Maybe a little."

"Doll face, do you really think Gram or Pop would knowingly take me or you anywhere that wasn't safe?"

"I suppose not," I mumbled.

Phoenix reached over and placed his hand on my thigh, giving it a reassuring squeeze. "There's nothing for you to worry about. I'll stay by your side the whole time if you want me to."

"Okay, Phoenix."

He seemed satisfied with my response, but I remained a ball of nerves for the rest of the journey.

When we pulled through the gates to the compound, Gram and Pop were already out of their car and hugging or shaking hands with various leather-clad men.

Phoenix took my hand and approached the sea of leather as if he didn't have a care in the world, and I guess he didn't.

"Phoenix, good to see you, boy," a man who looked very similar to Pop said as he pulled Phoenix into a hug. "And who do we have here?"

"Uncle Talon, this is my girlfriend, Annabelle.

Annabelle, this is Pop's brother and president of the Blackwings Motorcycle Club, Talon Black."

I carefully extended my hand and squeaked in surprise when he engulfed me in a hug. "Pleasure to meet you, Annabelle. Merry Christmas."

"Uh, Merry Christmas to you, too, sir."

"A pretty girl with manners. You better hang on to her, Phoenix," Talon said.

"I plan to," Phoenix replied instantly.

"Follow me. I need to get back inside before Hawk's two hellions destroy the clubhouse."

We followed him inside to find two little boys who were undoubtedly up to something. They stood side by side with their hands behind their backs grinning at their grandfather.

"Boys, say hello to your cousin and his girlfriend, Annabelle."

Both boys said in unison, "Hey, Phoenix," but never glanced his way. They kept their eyes fixed on me.

"Hello, Annabelle," one of them said, stepping closer to me and reaching for my hand. He placed a kiss on top of my hand and continued, "A beautiful name for a beautiful girl. I'm Copper Black, and I must say it is a pleasure to meet you."

Not to be outdone, the other boy took my hand

and placed two kisses to the top of it. "Hello, Annabelle. I'm Bronze Black. Welcome to the clubhouse. May I offer you something to drink? Perhaps a snack? Somewhere to sit?"

"Good gravy," Talon muttered while shaking his head. "Hawk!" he yelled. "Come get your spawn before I let Phoenix crack their skulls together for hitting on his girl in front of him!"

A man looking just like the rest of the Black men appeared and put a hand on each boy's head. "You two go play outside and for fuck's sake, stay out of trouble!"

Both boys winked at me before they ran off as instructed. "Sorry about those two. They're a handful. You must be Annabelle. I'm Hawk Black, Talon's son," he said and extended his hand.

I shook his hand and asked, "How old are your boys?"

"They're nine years old. I don't know what we're going to do when they're teenagers."

"Oh, I didn't realize they were twins."

Hawk laughed. "They're Irish twins, not traditional twins."

"Irish twins?"

"Yeah, Bronze was born early, so they're only eight months apart," he explained.

Our conversation was interrupted by a woman's piercing scream. "Goldie!" Hawk yelled and took off down the hall followed by Talon.

Talon stormed past us moments later and straight out the front door. He came back inside with Copper's upper arm in one hand and Bronze's upper arm in the other.

Phoenix wrapped his arm around my shoulders and pulled me close. "Just watch, baby," he whispered.

Hawk returned to the common room carrying two snakes. I tried to turn and make a dash for the front door, but Phoenix held me tightly to him.

"Boys! I told you to make sure their cage was latched. I promised your mother this very thing wouldn't happen. If Slither and Squeeze get out again, they're gone. Go put them up and for the love of all that is holy, make sure the top is latched!" Hawk ordered before handing the snakes to Copper and Bronze.

The boys disappeared down the hall, and Hawk turned to the room to explain. "Goldie was going to take a short nap before lunch. Found the new pets curled up under the heating blanket on our bed."

Talon chuckled. "I told you not to get them

those snakes. You knew something like this would happen. Though, I am surprised it happened so fast. They've had them, what? Two? Three hours?"

Hawk rolled his eyes, but otherwise ignored his father.

I turned to Phoenix and quietly asked, "Those snakes are going to be here, inside the clubhouse?"

"Yeah, doll face, they are, but there's no reason to be scared. One, I highly doubt those snakes will get out again today. Two, even if they did escape again, they're ball pythons and won't hurt you."

"You can't be serious?"

"I am. A lot of people have them as pets. They're non-venomous and they aren't big enough to kill humans by constriction. Well, they might be able to kill a baby, but we don't have any of those around so it's not an issue."

"I'm not sure I believe you," I said hesitantly.

He grinned and reached into his pocket. "Here," he said and handed me his pocket knife. "Keep that with you. If one of the snakes gets out and wraps around your neck, use my knife to cut it."

My eyes widened in surprise. Phoenix just

laughed and said, "Trust me, doll face. We won't see those snakes again during our visit. Copper and Bronze have been begging for pet pythons for the last two Christmases, and they know their mom will make them get rid of them if they escape again."

I believed him, but I still jumped and flinched with every unexpected touch, from an actual person or when my clothes wrinkled against my skin for the next few hours.

When we sat down for dinner, I felt much more comfortable with the bikers surrounding me. I was amazed at how easily these men of no blood relation formed a family. And that's what it was, a family. A family I looked forward to being a part of.

I joined Phoenix's family for New Year's as well. I don't know if my mother didn't realize I wasn't home for any of the major holidays or if she was too out of it to realize it was the holidays. Either way, I enjoyed the holiday season for the first time in my life.

After the holidays, my life at home was marginally better. My father continued to drop in unannounced every two weeks or so and my mother continued to drink herself into a coma on a daily basis. I often wondered where she got the money since she wasn't working that I knew of, but ultimately figured I was better off not knowing.

As the months passed, I fell more and more in love with Phoenix. We spent many evenings and nights with just the two of us making our plans for the future. He would join the Marines after graduation while I would stay in Croftridge and continue to work at the shop with Gram. I was hoping to get a scholarship and take some classes at the local community college while he was away. When he returned home after his first deployment, we would get married, and I would either move to the base with him, move in with Gram and Pop, or maybe even share an apartment with Macy—anything to get me away from my parents until Phoenix and I could be together all the time.

Little did either of us know, we didn't have the luxury of waiting for him to return to Croftridge. No, after his plane took off, our plans crumbled in the wind.

CHAPTER SEVEN

Annabelle

Phoenix had been gone for a little over three weeks, and I was dying to talk to him. I needed to talk to him. He told me he wouldn't be able to call often, and it was even more difficult for me to talk to him because I didn't have a phone. The two times he had called his Gram's shop, I hadn't been there. Those two times had been on a Tuesday. So, when the next Tuesday rolled around, I was bound and determined to be in the shop.

I opened the front door, ready to climb on my bicycle and pedal to work two hours early, to find a familiar yet unexpected guy standing on the front porch, poised and ready to knock.

"Octavius, what are you doing here?" I asked.

I remembered him from school, though I didn't know him very well. We weren't friends, but we did have one or two classes together. Still, there was no reason for him to be at my house.

"Hello, Annabelle. I'm here to speak to your father."

"He's not here right now," I said, confused as to why he would be asking for my father.

"Yes, I am, stupid girl," my father grunted from behind me, causing me to jolt in surprise.

Octavius cleared his throat. "May I come in?"

"Get the fuck out of the way and go to your room, girl," my father ordered as he shoved me toward the hall.

"I was just leaving. I have to work today," I said quietly.

"Go to your fucking room!" he bellowed.

My father had never raised a hand to me, but I highly suspected that had more to do with the fact that he was rarely ever home and less to do with his moral compass. Regardless, I wasn't going to test my theory, so I scurried to my room as ordered.

My stomach churned as I waited in my room. I could hear Octavius and my father talking, but I couldn't make out what they were saying. I had a bad feeling and no amount of pacing or nail chewing was doing anything to alleviate it.

The knock on my bedroom door startled me. Before I could walk across the room and open it, my father flung it open and barged into my room. "You're coming with us," he told me and grabbed my arm. "Let's go."

Instinctively, I pulled against his grip. "Let go! What are you talking about?" I yelled.

"Stop fighting me and get your ass in the car!" he bellowed as he drug me out of the house kicking and screaming. I was certain he was on some kind of drugs. We didn't even have a car.

He roughly tossed me into the back seat of a large SUV. Inside, I found my mother in her drunken haze sitting beside Octavius, who was creepily smiling at me.

I pushed myself up and dove for the still open door. My father slammed it shut, narrowly missing my face, and then I heard the unmistakable sound of the doors locking.

I whirled around. "What in the hell is going on?" I screamed.

My mother didn't so much as twitch, despite my screaming. Octavius, however, casually leaned back in his seat, propping his elbows beside the headrests. "Allow me to explain, Annabelle. You see, your parents borrowed quite a large sum of money from me and have been unable to pay it back. As per our agreement, your parents must work off their debt on my family's dairy farm. To prevent people from trying to skip out on their debt, I require them, as well as their families, to live on the property until the debt is paid off."

No. No, no, no, no, no. "What about my stuff? I need my clothes and all of my other things!" I was grasping at straws, but I thought if I could get him to let me go back inside the house, I could figure out a way to get away from him. If I could just get to Gram and Pop, they would help me.

"I'll arrange for some of my men to pack up your belongings and have them delivered to your room on the property."

"What about my job? I have to be at work in an hour!" I shrieked.

"You won't be working anywhere other than the farm."

"No!" I screamed and lunged for him. I wrapped my hands around his throat and managed to get in two good shakes before I was pulled away and forcefully placed in the rear row of seating.

Octavius cleared his throat and smoothed his rumpled shirt. "I would advise you not to try anything like that again. This is your only warning."

"Fuck you," I spat.

He sighed in exasperation. "Fine. Have it your way." He raised his hand in the air and made some gesture. Suddenly, two men came at me. Asshole One cuffed my hands behind my back while Asshole Two placed a gag in my mouth and fastened my seatbelt.

"You'll learn, Annabelle. If you do as I say, things will go smoothly, but I will not tolerate disrespect from you or anyone else."

Well, I was in for a bumpy ride because there was no way in hell I would ever respect a little weasel like him.

CHAPTER EIGHT

Phoenix

When I stepped onto the front porch, I wasn't sure if I should knock or not. It was technically still my home, but it felt strange to walk right in since I hadn't lived there in almost a year. Plus, Gram and Pop weren't expecting me. Had they known I was back from deployment and coming home for a few weeks, they would have met me at the airport.

I knocked on the door as I pushed it open. "Anybody home?" I called out.

"Phoenix!!" Gram shrieked and came at me full speed ahead. "Why didn't you tell us you were coming home?" she asked as she cried against my shoulder. "Let me get a look at you. You're not hurt, are you?"

"No, Gram. I'm just fine. I didn't tell you because I wanted it to be a surprise. I have a few weeks of leave before I have to be back at the base."

"Come on in the kitchen and let me make you something to eat. Oh, I need to call Pop and tell him your home," she rambled as she made her way to the kitchen. "He had to run some papers into town, but he should be on his way back by now."

When she finally took a breath, I asked, "Gram, where's Annabelle?" I hadn't been able to talk to her since the day I left, and I was anxious to see her or at least hear her voice. When I left, she didn't have a phone and refused to let me buy her one. Instead, we'd planned on me calling the store to chat with her and Gram when they were both working. However, every time I called, Annabelle was either not working or had just stepped out.

Gram turned around to face me and the look on her face had my blood turning to ice. She slowly approached the table and sat down beside me, grabbing my hand with hers. "Sweetheart," she said and her voice cracked. "We don't know where she is. We tried to—"

"What the fuck do you mean you don't know where she is?" I roared, jumping to my feet and knocking the kitchen chair over.

Gram's sniffles turned into sobs. The front door flew open, and there was Pop. "Phoenix Alexander Black, sit your ass down and apologize to your Gram. You know better than to take that tone with her!"

"Gram, I-I'm sorry. I just…I don't understand. Where is she?" I asked, desperate for any morsel of information.

"Phoenix," Pop said, taking a seat beside Gram. "We don't know where she is. After you left, everything was fine for a few weeks. Then, one day she didn't show up for work at the shop. We knew she didn't have a phone, so I rode out to her house to check on her. No one came to the door, and it looked like no one was home. Macy showed up at the shop that afternoon to take Annabelle home from work and was equally concerned when we told her what was going on. She promised to call if she heard from Annabelle, and we promised to do the same. I went back to the house for the next two days with no luck. I did get the guys at the police station to let me file a missing person's report, though there wasn't much they could do other than monitor the property for activity. Since her parents were gone, too, it appeared like the family moved. I even checked with the post office to see if they left a forwarding address. I wanted answers, and I knew you would, too, so, after I left the police station, I called a friend of mine who's a private investigator, and he's been looking for her and her family ever since."

"Why didn't you tell me?" I asked, barely managing to contain my anger. It wasn't Pop's fault, or Gram's, but I was furious, and I was close to taking it out on them.

"Because we love you. Think about it, Phoenix. If we told you Annabelle had disappeared while you were overseas, it would have been hell on you to know you were stuck over there and couldn't do a thing about it. You would have likely gotten yourself killed or court-martialed. I made the decision to keep it from you for your own good, and I'm not sorry for it." He paused for a moment and softened his tone, "And a part of me thought we would find her and have her here with us by the time you got back. I'm so sorry, my boy."

I nodded in acknowledgment, keeping my eyes on my clasped hands in my lap. Slowly taking in a deep breath, I rose to my feet. "I'm going to head out for a bit. I need some time to myself."

I moved next to Gram. "I'm sorry for raising my voice at you. I'll be back a little later." With that, I kissed her cheek and headed for my bike.

Pop and Uncle Talon helped me get a motorcycle for my 18th birthday, despite Gram's valiant protests. From the moment I got it, Annabelle and I were on my bike every chance we got. As I rode to Annabelle's house, I could almost feel her arms around me, could almost feel her laughter being carried away by the wind.

I parked my bike in her driveway, walked right up to her front door, and started banging on it. After several rounds of knocking and waiting, I walked to each window and peered inside. Months had passed since I left, yet it appeared no one was, or had been, living there.

When I came to the flimsy back door, I eyed it for a few brief moments before deciding I didn't give a shit and kicked the fucker open with my booted foot. I stepped into the house I had only been in a few times before and surveyed the area. What little had once been in the house was completely gone. Still, I refused to believe what I was seeing.

Upon entering Annabelle's room, the truth

finally hit me like a battering ram. She was gone. She'd been gone for months, just like Pop said, judging by the layer of dust on the window sill. Her room was completely bare, not a single piece of evidence to prove she ever lived in this space.

I lost it. I threw punch after punch and kick after kick into the walls until I couldn't feel my hands or feet anymore. Stumbling back into the wall, I clutched my chest and tried desperately to breathe. I slid down the wall until my ass hit the floor. Sucking in a large breath, I screamed my pain into the stale air while rivers of tears streamed down my face.

She was gone.

My Annabelle was gone.

Hours passed.

The tears finally ran dry.

I remained on the floor.

I couldn't bring myself to leave the last place where I had any hope of finding her. In my mind, if I left, it would all be real. As long as I was there waiting for her, she would come back. She would know I was there and come back.

Pop found me on the floor of her bedroom well after the sun had gone down. He silently sat down beside me and placed his arm around my shoulders. He never once asked me if I was okay or told me I needed to leave. He just waited with me until I was able to walk out of that house by my own choice, which ended up being around 7:00 am the next morning.

Gram was waiting for us on the front porch, nervously pacing back and forth. When I was within arm's reach, she hugged me tightly and tried to ease the pain of my broken heart. Nothing short of finding Annabelle would take away any of the pain.

"Phoenix, honey, your hands," Gram gasped. "I think we need to go to the hospital."

"Let him be, love. The only thing hurting him right now is his heart, and there's nothing the hospital can do for that," Pop said.

I left them on the porch and stumbled to my room in a daze. I managed to get a few hours of sleep before I set out and scoured the town. I asked anyone and everyone I could find about Annabelle and her parents. No one had any answers. I tried to track down Macy, but Pop told me she moved away after she and Aaron broke up and Annabelle disappeared. Pop said he still talked to her every now and then, but he waited for her to call him because it was hard for her to talk about Annabelle.

I spent the entire two weeks of my leave

relentlessly searching for any clues as to what happened to my girl. I was devastated when my time was up and I had to return to base. I needed more time to search. I considered taking my chances and not returning, but Pop convinced me otherwise by promising to continue searching for her in my absence.

So, with a tearful goodbye, I left my grandparents' house and returned to base not knowing what happened to the love of my life.

CHAPTER NINE

Annabelle

I woke up feeling like crap. My back was killing me and the stupid Braxton-Hicks contractions wouldn't let up. "Slightly uncomfortable" my ass. These fuckers hurt. To top it off, apparently, I peed in the bed while I was sleeping. Heaving myself out of bed, I waddled to the bathroom and quickly realized two things. I hadn't peed in the bed, and I wasn't having Braxton-Hicks contractions.

Wrapping my arms around my large belly, I doubled over in pain when the next contraction hit. As soon as I was able to take a breath, I screamed, "Octavius!"

He walked into the bathroom attached to my

bedroom and studied me. His eyes held nothing but contempt. "What is it, Annelle?"

Was he fucking serious? "It's time, Octavius. The baby is coming," I gritted out.

He nodded. "Well, let's get you over to see the doctor," he said, sounding bored.

He took his sweet time covering the car seat with trash bags so I didn't ruin the interior of his car with my "fluids of life," his words, not mine. If I physically could have, I would have kneed him in the balls. Could he not tell I was in a significant amount of pain and needed medical attention ASAP? Of course, he could; he just didn't care. I don't know why I thought he might have some sort of compassion for me.

When we arrived at the clinic on the farm, I waddled inside without any assistance from Octavius. He walked right past the receptionist and through the door that led to the patient rooms in the back of the clinic, leaving me standing in the waiting room clutching my stomach and grunting with each contraction.

He returned a few minutes later and instructed me to follow him. He led me to a room in the very back corner of the clinic. It looked more like Dr. Frankenstein's lab than any clinic room I had ever seen before.

"Climb up on the table, Annelle," the doctor said.

"In case you haven't noticed, that's physically impossible for me to do at this time," I snapped.

Octavius huffed. "Oh, fine. Just try not to drip on me," he muttered in disgust as he reached under my arms to lift me onto the table.

I can't say what happened next was my finest moment, but he deserved it and so much more. The moment my feet were off the ground, I pretended to have another contraction while I emptied my bladder all over his legs and feet.

He dropped me onto the table and started dancing around, squealing in horror. I barely managed to contain my laughter while I watched him hurry to remove his piss soaked socks and shoes.

I should have been paying attention to the doctor and not Octavius. Had I been, I would have seen him walking toward me with a syringe in his hand.

He jabbed the needle in my arm and said, "Annelle, I'm going to put you to sleep. You need to have a C-section." I don't know what he gave me, but I was rapidly succumbing to it. I didn't even get a chance to ask how he knew I needed to have a C-section without examining me first.

When I woke, I was in a lot of pain, and my mind felt cloudy. I tried to sit up, but was quickly pushed back down by a large, cold hand. "You can't get up right now, Annelle," Octavius said.

"Where's my baby? Did everything go okay?" I asked.

He smiled at me. He never smiled. A sick feeling washed over me. Something was wrong. I just knew it.

When he continued to smile at me, I demanded, "Tell me where my baby is!"

"I'm sorry, Annelle. Your little girl was stillborn. The doctor tried to resuscitate her, but he said she had been gone too long," Octavius said in an almost jovial tone.

A little girl.

I had a little girl.

Had.

Had.

HAD.

"I want to see her!"

"Unfortunately, that's not possible. We've already removed the carcass from the premises."

I slapped him across the face using every bit of strength I had. "Don't you ever call my baby a carcass again, you sadistic son of a bitch."

I slumped back into the bed. My physical pain

was all but forgotten as I was consumed with an agony I didn't know existed. A hurt so great, no one should ever have to feel it. My little girl didn't make it. I did everything I could to make sure she was healthy. What went wrong? What did I do? How was I going to continue living without her? Why would I want to? I didn't even get to hold her. I didn't get to see her. I felt like I was suffocating as unanswered questions and powerful emotions consumed me. I couldn't breathe. I didn't want to breathe.

I vaguely heard Octavius saying something. Then, the doctor appeared beside my bed and put something into my IV. Moments later, I slipped into the darkness, in more ways than one.

CHAPTER TEN

Annabelle

Six weeks later

"Annelle, need I remind you again that you agreed to this? I've been patient, but it's time to have the wedding ceremony so we can get you pregnant. The doctor said we could start trying to conceive a child six weeks after your delivery. It's been six weeks today. You can participate willingly, or not, I don't really care," Octavius said.

Annelle. I hated that fucking name, especially hearing his smarmy ass say it. Turning to face him, I smiled cruelly. "I've had time to give this some thought. I never agreed to marry you. I did agree to bear you a son, but I never agreed to be your wife or have sexual intercourse with you."

He blanched. "What exactly are you saying?"

My smile grew even wider. "I'm saying I won't marry you, and there is no way in hell I will allow you to stick your dick in me. If you want me to carry your child, you need to find a cup with a lid and a magazine you'll enjoy."

"Watch it. I can make your life a living hell, Annelle."

"You already have. But fine, go ahead and go back on your word. I'll be more than happy to tell anyone and everyone around here who will listen about how you don't stand by what you promise."

"Fuck!" he screamed and slammed the door as he left the room.

I knew that would get him. He had some serious hang-ups, and one of those was being true to his word. He never specified the manner in which a son would be conceived. I agreed to give him a son, but I never agreed to give him my body. My body belonged to only one man, as well as my heart.

He returned several days later to take me to the clinic. I hated that fucking place with a passion. If I ever got the chance, I would set it on fire and watch it burn to the ground.

"Why did you bring me here?" I asked the asshole beside me.

"To get the process started for in vitro fertilization. As you pointed out, you agreed to give me a son, but did not agree to sexual intercourse. You also did not agree to give me a daughter. This method will ensure a son is implanted in your womb."

Eight weeks later, tests confirmed I was pregnant with the spawn of Satan after one round of IVF. Eight months later, I gave birth to a healthy baby boy via C-section, one I was actually conscious for, though I would've preferred not to be.

I tried, I really did, to love that little baby boy, but I could barely stand to look at him. I made sure he was cared for and well taken care of, but I didn't hold him or spend any time with him when I didn't have to. Funny thing was, as much as I thought I didn't love him, I couldn't find it in myself to leave him behind, either.

CHAPTER ELEVEN

Annabelle

Thirteen years ago

"Did you text him?" I asked. I was a nervous wreck. I just knew something was going to go wrong and I couldn't afford for anything to go wrong. If it did, I would never get an opportunity like this again.

"I did, and he replied back. Everything is all set and they're expecting us," Kathleen replied. "I can't imagine what you're feeling right now, but try to calm down a little. My brother is very good at what he does. He'll take care of you. I promise."

I wanted to believe her, but I was afraid to hope. My life had been a miserable existence for the last six years. This was my one chance to get me and my son away from Octavius and start a new life.

Kathleen and her husband lived on the farm property. Kathleen worked part-time as a secretary in the dairy farm's office, and her husband was a full-time dairy farm employee. They also had a little boy named Coal who was about a year older than Nivan.

After years of building a relationship with Kathleen, I finally found the courage to ask her if she would help me escape. I explained to her that I didn't live on the farm by my own choice, and Octavius was keeping me there after he forced me to have his child. She was shocked at first, but readily agreed to help me.

As luck would have it, Kathleen's brother, Luke, was a federal agent and had the resources to make people disappear. Kathleen convinced him to help me while keeping it under the radar. He formulated a plan and made all of the arrangements. We needed to wait for Octavius to be out of town on a business trip, then we just had to show up at the designated location.

The morning of my planned escape, I showed

up at Kathleen's house with Nivan and a fairly large box. She opened the door and eyed the box curiously while she ushered us into her house.

"I know I can't take anything with me, but there were a few things I couldn't bear to leave with Octavius. Will you do something with them for me? It's really not that much. I put some of Nivan's toys on top of my things, in case anybody asked to look in the box. And there's no reason Coal shouldn't have them since we can't take them with us," I explained.

Kathleen gave me a sad smile. "Thank you, Anelle. I'll take care of your things for you."

When we arrived at the Cedar Valley Emergency Department, Kathleen carried Nivan and helped me inside. She told them she found me on the side of the road. I was doing my best to act like I had a head injury and couldn't talk. Kathleen was holding my son in her lap and quietly reminding him to not answer any questions. She followed along as I was placed in a room and registered as Jane Doe.

Luke had a friend who was a resident at Cedar Valley Regional Hospital. He was watching for a Jane Doe to show up in the Emergency Department. He was assigned as my doctor, and when the coast was clear, he led me to an exit at the back of the hospital while avoiding all security cameras.

At the back of the hospital, a blacked out SUV was waiting by the loading dock. I climbed into the back and was whisked away to a private airfield several hours from Cedar Valley. From there, I was flown to California, where Luke had set up my new life. He had a fully furnished house waiting for me, a new identity, money to get started on, and even a job.

I don't think I took a full breath until I closed the front door of my new house and set the security alarm. Then, I exhaled that full breath and dropped to my knees in tears. I was utterly relieved to finally be away from Octavius and his evil ways, but I was beyond devastated that my new life meant Phoenix could never be a part of it. For me, that was the hardest part about leaving. I loved that man with my whole heart, and I was having a hard time accepting that he was forever lost to me.

In a way, I was also lost. I was no longer Annabelle Burnett, the girl from Croftridge who fell in love with her high school sweetheart and planned to marry him and have his babies. Now, I was Taylor Davis, a new resident of northern California, and I had no idea who she was.

PART TWO

CHAPTER TWELVE

Phoenix

Present Time

I sat at my desk going through yet another stack of papers found in one of the hidden rooms on the farm property. Octavius kept meticulous records, which created a lot of paperwork. It had taken me almost a year to get through the better part of it, and I still had nothing on Annabelle.

I tossed the current papers I was holding in the shredder and moved to the next folder in the stack. When I opened it, my breath caught in my chest. I closed my eyes and slowly opened them again, not believing what I was seeing. At the top of the first paper in the folder was the name I had been searching for.

Annabelle Burnett.

My hands were shaking as I carefully placed the folder on my desk and began looking through it. My heart was pounding in my chest, blood whooshing in my ears as I looked at the contents of the folder. The first things I saw were Annabelle's birth certificate and social security card. Behind that, I found birth records for Ember, Coal, and Nivan. Then, Nivan's death certificate. Though, it was the next few papers that caught me by surprise.

There were two hospital reports, one for a Jane Doe and the other for a Johnny Doe, admitted to Cedar Valley Regional Emergency Department. I carefully read through the reports.

A woman and a young boy were found on the side of the road. The woman appeared to have some sort of head trauma and was unable to answer any questions. The young boy refused to talk to any of the hospital staff. The woman was sent for a CT scan of her head, but never arrived in the Radiology Department. According to the reports, the woman was nowhere to be found, assumed to have left against medical advice, and the young boy was found dead in his hospital bed. Both reports had the same date as the date on Nivan's death certificate.

The name of the physician who had written the report caught my eye. After reading it twice to be sure I wasn't mistaken, I picked up my phone and placed a call. Each ring was excruciatingly long until he finally picked up. "Patch, get your ass in my office right now!"

***

When Patch arrived, I handed him the report and immediately started questioning him. He was reluctant at first, but finally told me Luke Johnson had asked him to take that particular case. There was nothing actually wrong with the woman; her coming to the hospital was just a means to help her escape.

"I swear, Prez, if I had known it was Annabelle, or even thought it was, I would've told you. When I joined the club and heard you talking about your past, it never occurred to me that the woman I helped could have been your girl. I never knew her name. I didn't even know where she came from. Luke said it was better that way, plausible deniability and all that."

"Relax," I said. "I'm not pissed at you. I just

want to know what you know so I can fucking find her."

"That's really about it. I ordered a CT scan for her. When it was time for the test, I volunteered to take her to Radiology. Instead, I led her to the back of the hospital where a car was waiting. She got in, and I went back inside. I don't know what happened after that," he explained.

"So, the boy wasn't found dead in his hospital room?"

Confusion washed over Patch's face. "What boy?"

"The boy who came to the hospital with her. Her son," I said and handed him the other hospital report.

Patch looked over the paper. "I've never seen this report before. And I would certainly remember finding a young child dead in their hospital room."

"It has your name on it," I pointed out.

"Well, it was fucking forged. I swear, Phoenix, there was no child with her."

"It says right there that she arrived with a small child!" I yelled, stabbing my finger at the paper on my desk.

"I know what it says, Prez. I'm telling you, she didn't have a kid with her. Maybe Luke knew something I didn't."

"Yeah, okay. I'll see what I can get out of Luke. Thanks, brother." With that, Patch left my office, and I placed another call.

"Phoenix, what's up man?" Luke answered.

"Any chance you're around and can swing by the clubhouse?" I asked. I did not want to have this conversation over the phone, and I'm sure he didn't either.

"Sure. I'm in the city so it'll be about an hour or so. Is everything okay?" he asked, hesitantly.

"Yeah, man, it's nothing like last time."

"I'll be there as soon as I can," he said and disconnected.

When Luke sat down in my office, I slid the hospital reports over to him. He skimmed over the pages then returned his focus to me. "How did you get these?"

Instead of answering him, I pushed the file folder with Annabelle's name on it to him. He glanced at it and looked at me questioningly. "Those reports were in that folder. I found it while going through more of Octavius's stuff."

"And you think this is Annabelle? Your Annabelle?" he asked, eyes wide.

"Yes." I pulled out a picture of Annabelle when she was 18 years old and placed it on the desk in front of him. I knew he had seen her picture before, but I felt compelled to show him again. "Is this the girl you and Patch helped?"

He glanced at the picture and back to me. "I don't know. I never saw her. I made all the arrangements, but I was a few states away on an assignment when this happened. I had another agent meet her at the hospital."

"Get him on the phone. See if this is the girl," I demanded, shaking the picture at him.

Luke shook his head. "Can't. He was killed in the line of duty a few years ago." Luke's brows furrowed, and then his head shot up. "It can't be the same girl. You told me Annabelle disappeared in 1998. We helped this girl six years later."

"It could be if she was kidnapped and held against her will for six years," I pointed out.

"Fuck!" Luke swore. "Did you show that picture to Patch?"

Fuck me. I needed to take a deep breath and focus. Shaking my head, I reached for my phone. "Patch, brother, I need you back in my office."

When he arrived, I didn't even give him a chance to sit down. I was on my feet and in front of him holding up the picture of Annabelle. "Is this her? The girl you helped?"

His eyes widened, and then he paled as

recognition washed over his face. Slowly nodding his head, he carefully said, "Yes, Prez, that's her."

Jane Doe was Annabelle. My heart started to pound in my chest again. I closed my eyes in relief for a brief moment before opening them and pinning Luke with my gaze. "What happened to her? Where did you send her? Where is she now?" I began firing off questions faster than he could answer.

He held his hands up. "Hang on, Phoenix. I can't give you that information. It's federally classified. You know this."

"I'm guessing that means you also can't tell me anything about the boy."

He grimaced and shook his head. "Patch, you probably don't want to be present for the rest of this conversation."

Patch nodded in understanding and quickly left my office.

I slammed both hands down on the desk making Luke flinch back. "I don't give a fuck if it's classified information or not, you need to start talking! That is the love of my life, and she has two children here that are alive and well. My children. They at least deserve a chance to meet their own freaking mother!" I roared.

"Phoenix, calm down. I'm not saying I won't help you, I'm just saying I can't straight out tell you exactly where she is," he hedged.

"Start helping," I ordered through gritted teeth. I had no patience left. He knew where my girl was, and he was going to tell me how to find her in the next few seconds or I was going to beat the living shit out of him, federal agent or not.

"You remember Wave?" he asked. I nodded. Of course, I remembered Wave. We all crossed paths at some point when we were active Marines. The last I heard, Wave was the president of his own motorcycle club, the Knights of Neptune out on the west coast. "Maybe you should go visit Wave. Take some time to catch up with him and hang around the city. See what life in his little slice of Heaven is like."

"Thanks, man. You have no idea..." I trailed off, unable to formulate the right words. He basically told me where to find my Annabelle. Words couldn't convey how much that meant to me.

"I do," he said. "When are you heading out?"

"As soon as fucking possible. Been looking for that girl for 19 years. I'm not wasting another second," I declared.

CHAPTER THIRTEEN

Phoenix

Ileft to go find my girl the very next morning. I told the officers in Church what I was doing, but they were given strict instructions to keep their mouths shut. I didn't want Ember or Coal getting wind of it and following me out to California. We told everyone else, including Ember and Coal, that I would be gone on a run for two to three weeks to discuss a new business opportunity with an old friend.

I rode from sunup to sundown as fast as I could, only stopping for a quick bite to eat and to refuel. At night, I found the closest motel and crashed until morning. It only took me three days to make it to the small coastal town of Rocky

Point in northern California. I found a cheap motel and booked a room for the next week.

After washing the road off and getting something to eat, I had to force myself to go to bed. I was tired, but knowing that I was likely in the same town as my Annabelle was making it difficult, to say the least, to fall asleep. I finally managed to get a handle on my excitement and got a few hours of rest.

The next morning, I wasn't sure where to start. I didn't want to go straight to Wave and ask for his help. For some reason, I wanted to find her myself. I couldn't explain it, but it was just something I felt I had to do.

The town really wasn't that big. It took me less than an hour to circle the whole town and ride up and down every major road. Once I had a feel for the lay of the land, it was time to start searching.

I sat down at a booth in the back of a little cafe on the main street of Rocky Point, aptly named Rocky Point Cafe. With a fresh cup of coffee in front of me and a hearty breakfast on its way, I tried to think of places where I could find her. She had to have a job, but I had no idea what it could be. She could be anything at this point. She'd had plenty of time to go to school and get a college education.

Staring into the cup of coffee I held between both of my hands, I wracked my brain trying to come up with job possibilities for Annabelle. My head jerked up when the waitress brought my breakfast plate over, and my eyes landed on a very distinct piece of artwork hanging on the wall. "Excuse me, ma'am, do you happen to know where that came from?" I asked, pointing to the picture on the wall.

She smiled and batted her lashes at me. "Yes, I do. That was created by a local artist by the name of Taylor Davis."

"If I wanted to purchase something by that artist, where could I find more of their work?" I asked. I wasn't sure what, but something about the art was calling to me. I couldn't take my eyes off of it.

"Taylor works down at the tattoo shop, The Inkwell. They've got some of Taylor's work for sale hanging in the front of the shop, or you can have something custom done for you."

"Thank you," I said, dismissing her and tucking into my breakfast.

Figuring The Inkwell was as good a place as any to start my search, I decided to go there after breakfast. On my way out, I stopped at the door to look at the picture a little closer. I had never been that drawn to artwork before. I was just about to put the whole thing out of my mind when I saw it. In the corner, by the artist's signature, was a tiny little phoenix. My phoenix.

Suddenly, I was assaulted by a flood of memories. Annabelle drawing the same little phoenix on my hand during one of our dates. Annabelle doodling the same phoenix all over her notebooks. Me giving her custom made earrings and a matching necklace of the same phoenix. Annabelle drawing a larger, more detailed version of that phoenix on paper and giving it to me for Christmas. Annabelle loved to draw and was damn good at it, too. After seeing it, I had no doubt in my mind the artist known as Taylor Davis was indeed Annabelle Burnett.

The Inkwell was easy enough to find. Luckily, there were several other businesses around and a few of them had benches out front. I took a seat and watched the shop from afar. It wasn't long before I spotted a petite woman with an odd mixture of black and blonde hair falling well past her shoulders inside the shop. She moved around with a confidence I hadn't ever seen in Annabelle. Her body and size matched what I imagined Annabelle's would be, but the hair color was different, though it could have been dyed. If I could get a look at her face, I would know for sure.

The woman disappeared into the back of the shop for long periods of time before reappearing near the front. Each time, she never looked toward the front of the shop. After several hours of trying to catch a glimpse of her face, I decided to go back to my hotel room for a few hours and come back in the evening. I didn't want to draw attention to myself, and I would do just that if I continued to sit on a bench and stare at the woman through the window. My exhaustion was catching up with me, despite my best efforts to ignore it, and I needed to catch up on some rest before I went back and tried to see her face. I could have just walked into the shop and asked to speak to her, but I needed to know it really was her before I went inside. I knew I couldn't handle it if it turned out the woman in the window wasn't my Annabelle.

CHAPTER FOURTEEN

Annabelle

I heard the bell on the front door ding. I looked up to see Nathan striding toward me with a huge grin on his face. "Can I assume from the smile on your face that everything went well?"

He beamed even brighter. "You sure can, Mom. I made it!" He picked me up for a hug and spun me around before putting my feet on the ground again.

I laughed. "You're going to have to stop doing that, son. I'm getting too old to be jostled around by a brute your size, and I have a feeling you're only going to get bigger."

"You're only 37 years old. That isn't anywhere near old," he replied.

"Talk to me when you're 37," I retorted. I refrained from adding, "And have been through all the shit I've been through." He didn't know about our past. What little he did remember was easily explained away by me. He was under the impression that his father died when he was a baby, and we moved to another part of California a few years later. He thought we had always lived on the west coast. He had no idea we were from a little town located in the foothills of the Great Smoky Mountains.

"You ready to go?" he asked.

"Yep. Wave, I'm leaving!" I shouted to my boss, who also happened to be one of my closest friends.

Wave got up and enveloped me in a hug, the same thing he did every day when I left the shop. He gave Nathan a man hug and patted him on the back. "Heard you talking to your momma. Congratulations, boy! I know how hard you've worked, and we're all proud of you!"

"Thanks, Uncle Wave. I couldn't have done it without you guys helping me train." He paused and lowered his voice, "If I do this, you'll be sure to look after Mom, right? I can't leave her alone."

I gasped. My sweet, sweet boy was worried about me. I cut in before Wave could answer,

"Nathan, you don't need to worry about me. I'll be fine, and yes, Uncle Wave will look after me. This is an opportunity I will not allow you to pass up. Do you understand me?" I asked in my mom voice with my hands on my hips.

"All right, Mom, you win," he sighed and headed toward the door.

"See ya later, Wave," I called over my shoulder, following after my son.

As soon as I stepped outside, I knew something wasn't right. My heart rate picked up and goosebumps covered my skin. I distractedly took the helmet from my son's outstretched hand and placed it on my head. Oblivious to my current state, he climbed onto the bike. I secured my helmet and climbed on behind him. The feeling I had intensified, and it felt like holes were burning into my left side. I turned my head and scanned the area, but I didn't see anything out of the ordinary. Still, I fisted Nathan's shirt and inhaled deeply.

Nathan turned his head back as far as he could. "Mom, what's wrong? Are you okay?"

I tightened my hold on his shirt. "Go, Nathan. Now!" I barked. Blessedly, he didn't question me. He took off like a bat out of hell, flying down the road, weaving in and out of traffic.

At some point, he must have turned on the Bluetooth communication because suddenly his voice filled my ears. "Where do you want me to go, Mom?"

Where did I want him to go? Was anything actually wrong? I had no proof, but I couldn't shake the feeling I had dreaded for years. The feeling of knowing we'd been found. Giving in to my delusions, I frantically shouted into my helmet, "Home, we have to go home!"

"Mom, tell me what's going on!" Nathan pleaded, his concern evident in his voice.

"I don't know. I'm mean, I'm not sure anything is going on. It's just a feeling. Just get us to the house and do as I say. If I'm right, we don't have time to waste." I hadn't worried about this day in years. I had gotten comfortable with our life. After five years of living in California with no problems, I started to relax and continued to do so over the last eight years. I tried desperately to remember my backup plan from years ago. Token! I would pack our shit and call Token. We would go to the clubhouse. We would be safe there until we figured out what to do next.

I calmed slightly once I had a plan in place, but my nerves wouldn't even be halfway soothed until we were safely locked away at the clubhouse.

Over the years, Wave and Token had gained my trust. I eventually shared some of my past with them, though I never gave them any names or told them exactly where I was from. Token had known more than Wave in the beginning, but it wasn't much. After I opened up, Wave point blank told me if I ever felt like I was in danger, I was to get me and Nathan to the clubhouse as fast as possible and let them handle everything else.

"Nathan, when we get to the house, I need you to go inside and pack the essentials you would need for a week or so and anything sentimental you absolutely do not want left behind. Leave anything that can be easily replaced. Once you have your stuff together, start loading it into my car."

"Damn it, Mom," Nathan huffed in exasperation.

"Don't you cuss at me, son. I don't have time to explain. Just get your stuff, and then we're going to the clubhouse. I'll explain there. I promise."

When we pulled up to the house, I was off the bike and through the front door before Nathan could turn off the engine. Tearing through house like a mad woman, I started cramming things into suitcases, laundry baskets, trash bags, anything I could find. I couldn't believe how much stuff we had acquired in the last 13 years. I literally had nothing but the clothes I was wearing when I arrived.

My phone ringing startled me to the point of weakening my knees. I grabbed it and was not surprised in the least to see Token's name flashing across the screen. I was kind of surprised it took as long as it did for one of them to call. Knowing Nathan, he was probably on the phone with them as soon as I was inside the house.

"Hey, Token," I answered, completely out of breath.

"What in the fuck is going on, Taylor? You sound like you've been running a marathon. I've got your boy calling me scared as hell because of the way you're acting. Start talking, half pint," he ordered.

"I think I've been found!" I shouted into the phone. "I'm trying to get our stuff and get to the clubhouse."

Token's entire tone changed instantly, "Stay calm, squirt. I'll be there in five. You want to stay on the phone with me until I get there?"

"No, I can work faster without the phone."

"All right, I'm going to call Wave. See you soon."

The call disconnected, and I got back to packing. I was almost finished with my bedroom when I heard the rumble of a bike pull up in front of my house, shortly followed by another rumble. That meant Wave and Token had arrived. I sagged with relief. They would get us to the clubhouse, and everything would be okay.

Just as that thought entered my head, I heard shouting outside. Loud, angry shouting coming from more than two men. Fucking hell. I ran through the house and yanked open the front door. I took one step outside, and when my eyes connected with the steely blue ones that frequented my dreams, the world around me ceased to exist. I covered my mouth and nose with my hands and inhaled sharply with disbelief. It couldn't be, could it? Was it really him? I was too afraid to move, knowing if I took my eyes off him for one fraction of a second, he would disappear before my very eyes.

"Doll face," he breathed. Those words jolted me from my stupor. I leaped off the front steps and ran at him with everything I had.

"Phoenix," I cried as I launched myself into his arms. "Oh, God, Phoenix," I sobbed.

He held me against his chest with an unforgiving grip while my feet dangled in the air.

My arms wrapped tightly around his neck. It's a wonder either of us could breathe.

"Baby," he murmured with his lips pressed against my temple.

I heard another bike pull up and a bit of commotion, but I couldn't tear myself away from him long enough to see who it was or what was happening. I was lost in the comfort of his familiar scent, the safety of his strong arms, and the warmth of his body pressed against mine.

"What in the fuck is going on here?" Wave bellowed.

"This guy pulled up and said he was looking for someone named Annabelle. Said he wasn't leaving until he spoke to her. Then, Taylor comes flying out of the house, runs to him, and burst into tears," Token explained.

Phoenix gently placed me on my feet, and I tried to take a step back to wipe the tears from my face, but he held me firmly against his side. "Not ready to let go of you just yet, doll face," he said quietly.

I opened my mouth to start explaining to Wave when he exclaimed, "Holy shit. Is that Phoenix Black I see standing in front of me?"

"The one and only," Phoenix said, spreading his arms out wide to display himself. I leaned away from him to get a look at him. Damn, he was still sexy as sin.

"You two know each other?" Token asked, gesturing between Wave and Phoenix.

"Yeah," Wave answered. "Met in the Marines. He's also Copper Black's cousin." Wave directed his attention back to Phoenix. "It's been a long time, man, and it's good to see you, but what are you doing at Taylor's place? You two know each other?"

"Taylor," Phoenix muttered.

"Yeah," Wave pointed at me. "That's Taylor Davis, and this is her place."

"Her name is Annabelle Burnett," Phoenix insisted, "and there are quite a few things her and I need to discuss."

I felt the blood drain from my face. I was pretty sure I knew some of the things we needed to discuss, and I had no interest in talking about any of them, especially not with an audience.

"Oh, fuck me," Token blurted. "He's from—"

I cut him off. "Stop right there, Token. Yes is the answer to the question you didn't get to ask, but this isn't a discussion that needs to happen outside or in front of just anyone." I cast my eyes toward the front door just as Nathan stepped outside hoping Token would get my meaning.

"He's not *him* is he?" Token asked quietly.

I shook my head quickly. "No, he's not." He's the good guy, I thought to myself.

Wave stepped in. "Nathan, can you go inside and pack an overnight bag for you and Taylor? You two are staying at the clubhouse tonight." Nathan nodded and went into the house. "Before he comes back, is there any chance that anyone else has discovered her location or possibly followed you?"

"If you're talking about Octavius, then no, he's dead. Has been for over a year now."

My hand flew to my chest. "What?" I breathed. Octavius was dead? I suddenly felt very unsteady on my feet. My body swayed to the right. I reached out for Wave or Token to steady myself when I felt Phoenix wrap his muscular arms around me to hold me steady.

I couldn't help myself. I melted into his broad chest, my arms circling around his waist. He smelled just like I remembered, a mix of leather, spice, and something woodsy. Before I could stop it, another sob escaped, followed by a torrent of tears. I had missed him so damn much.

I felt my body being lifted and moved. Phoenix's deep voice whispered softly into my ear, "Just taking you inside, doll face."

Doll face. How I had longed to hear him call me that over the years. He called me doll face the first day we met and continued to do so the entire time we were a couple.

Phoenix gently placed me on my sofa and sat down beside me. Nathan came running into the room. "Mom! Mom! What's wrong?" my son frantically yelled. "What the fuck did you do to her?"

I felt Phoenix's body stiffen, but I had no idea why. I was in such a state, I couldn't even scold Nathan for his foul language.

"Nathan, calm down," Wave commanded. "Your momma's okay. You know neither Token nor I would ever let anything happen to her. She just got some shocking news, that's all."

I sniffled and looked up at my son. "I'm fine, honey. You know how I can get when I'm really tired. I'm sorry if I scared you."

He studied me for a long minute. "I'm not sure I believe you, but I'll drop it for now. Are we ready to go to the clubhouse?"

I wasn't sure how to answer that question. I needed to talk to Phoenix, and, honestly, I didn't want to go anywhere without him, but I knew Wave had a party planned to celebrate Nathan's new contract, and I didn't want to miss that either.

Making the decision for me, Wave answered, "I think it would be a good idea if we all went back to the clubhouse. That okay with you, Phoenix?"

"Sure, man. Whatever you think is best," Phoenix replied.

I went to the bathroom and freshened up my appearance, grabbed a few things for the night, and rejoined everyone in the living room, more nervous than I had been in years. I couldn't even begin to figure out how Phoenix found me and more importantly, why he found me.

I followed the men outside and glanced between the bikes. I desperately wanted to ride with Phoenix, to cling to his waist and bury my nose in his back. Phoenix leaned down and whispered into my ear, "Go ride with your boy. I'll be right behind you."

Reluctantly, I climbed on behind my son. I glanced back at Phoenix several times before I finally told Nathan I was ready. Once we were on the road, he started talking. "Mom, who is Phoenix?"

I sighed. This was not a conversation I wanted to have with my son. I had to choose my words carefully, particularly until I saw confirmation that Octavius was indeed dead. I didn't think for one second that Phoenix was lying to me, but I wanted proof. No, I needed proof.

"Phoenix is someone I knew in high school. I haven't spoken to anyone from my hometown in a very long time. I don't know why he's here, but you know Wave wouldn't have invited him to the clubhouse if he didn't trust him."

"So, if he is just some old friend of yours, why were you so upset?"

"Honey, I'd really rather not have this conversation while we're on your bike. Can we table this for now?" I asked.

He reluctantly agreed and we rode the rest of the way to the clubhouse in silence. My mind was flooded with memories from the past, memories that made my heart ache with the thoughts of what could have been.

CHAPTER FIFTEEN

Phoenix

I don't know how I managed to keep my bike upright as I followed Wave to his clubhouse. After almost 20 years, I finally found my Annabelle. Only, she wasn't my Annabelle anymore. She was an older version of my Annabelle going by the name of Taylor Davis. And she had a son. A son that wasn't my son. That thought had me grinding my teeth and tightening my grip on my handlebars.

My mind was flooded with questions I desperately needed answered. How could she have another child and leave two children behind? Was this kid Octavius's son or did someone else father that child? How old was he?

How in the hell did she end up under Wave's watch? Oh, fuck me, was Wave that kid's father?

By the time we pulled into what I assumed was Wave's clubhouse, I had managed to get myself all worked up. I wanted to throttle Annabelle and kiss her at the same time. How could I feel so relieved to have finally found her while simultaneously being so damn angry with her? I didn't have a strong handle on my emotions. Part of me wanted to head back to my hotel room and try this again the next day while the other part of me wanted to never let her out of my sight again. The latter part of me won that battle.

I followed Wave into his clubhouse. It appeared to be an old indoor storage building that he converted to house his brothers. It was pretty shabby looking from the outside, but the inside was a different story. The front doors opened into a large room with tables, sofas, a few pool tables, and a bar at the back of the room. "Welcome to the Knights of Neptune's Clubhouse, Phoenix."

"Thanks, man. Nice setup you got here."

"Follow me. You look like you could use a drink," he said over his shoulder as he made his way to the bar. He was wrong. I couldn't use a drink; I needed a whole fucking bottle.

Wave cleared his throat and clapped his

hands together one time. "Listen up, Knights. This here is a buddy of mine from back in my days as a Marine. He's also the president of the Blackwings Motorcycle Club, so you'll see him wearing his colors. You treat my friend with respect or you will be answering to me." He chuckled and added, "If he doesn't whoop your ass first. Now, everybody, give Phoenix a Knights' welcome." The men in the clubhouse hooted and hollered, raising their drinks in the air. The women clapped and cheered. I was not up for social hour. I was here for one thing and one thing only, Annabelle.

Wave handed me a shot of whiskey, which I immediately downed and shoved my glass back for a refill. "Listen, man, I don't know her whole story, and it isn't any of my business, but I have to know, are you putting Taylor in any danger by being here?"

Taylor. I would never get used to that name. I shook my head. "Not at all. I'm pretty sure I know why she's been hiding out here all these years, and I can assure you, that reason is no longer an issue." As far as everyone knew, Octavius was dead and gone, and I had the papers to prove it.

"All right. I know we've lost touch over the years, but I trust you, man. It's just, Taylor has become a part of our family, and we all look out for her. Not a one of the Knights would let anything happen to her," he explained.

I couldn't help the disdain in my tone. "She an Old Lady?"

Wave laughed. A full out belly laugh. "Are you serious? How well did you know her? That girl has never, and I mean never, had anything to do with any of the brothers. Hell, I've known her for 13 years, and I've never seen her give any man a second glance. Over the years, she's become a little sister to the guys."

I managed to maintain my mask of indifference, but the relief I felt was almost too much to hide. "What about the kid?"

"Nathan? He's a good boy. Loves his momma with everything he has. I don't know what business you have with Taylor, but if anyone is going to give you trouble, it's going to be Nathan, and that's just because he's going to try to protect her. It's always been just the two of them. Hell, it took a long time before he warmed up to anyone other than Token, and he was just a tiny little shit then."

"How old is he?"

"Just turned 18 about a month ago," he said.

I sucked in a sharp breath. He was just a

year, maybe not even that, younger than Ember and Coal. That meant, without a doubt, he was really Nivan.

Nathan.

Nivan.

I slammed my fist down onto the bar. "Fuck!" Motherfucking son of a bitch.

Silence fell over the bar, and all eyes turned to me. Wave clapped me on the shoulder. "Come on, man, let's go to my office. Prospect, hand me that bottle. No, you fuckhead, the good shit."

I followed Wave into his office and dropped into the first chair I spotted. He handed me the bottle, and I took several long pulls before I came up for air. "Thanks, man. Listen, I need to talk to Anna— I mean Taylor?"

He leaned back against his desk and studied me. "Well, that'd be up to her, but I'm not so keen on it given your current state."

I sighed. "Fuck, if it makes you feel better, you can stay, but I can't not talk to her." I sounded like a pussy, but I didn't give a fuck at that very moment. She was the only one who could answer my questions, and I was only going to make myself crazy the longer I waited to ask them.

"Okay. I'll go get her for you."

Wave returned with Annabelle in his wake.

She walked into the office and leaned against a wall that happened to be the place in the room farthest from me. The tension in the room was damn near palpable, and it was obvious something had shifted during the ride from her house to the clubhouse. She quietly said, "Wave said you wanted to talk to me."

I half-laughed, half-scoffed. "Something like that. He feels like he should stay. You want him to hear all the shit we have to talk about? And let me just tell you now, I know most of what happened and there's A LOT you don't know."

She shifted her weight from foot to foot and started fidgeting with the hem of her shirt. "Um, I'm not sure…"

Enough of this bullshit. "Look, you know damn well I would never do anything to hurt you, but this conversation is going to be emotionally charged. There's no other way it can go. There will be yelling and crying and who knows what else, but I swear I won't touch you unless it's to comfort you."

She nodded. "Okay then. Do you want to go to the room I'm staying in for this?"

"I think that would be best." I stood and waited for her to show me the way.

Wave caught her arm and whispered

something in her ear. She nodded, patted his chest, and whispered something back. Any other time I would have been thrilled that she had someone who watched over her so closely, but it was currently pissing me off. Yeah, I would probably yell at her and get angry with her, but I had also missed her, longed for her, loved her for over 20 fucking years. I damn sure wouldn't do anything to hurt her.

Finally, she started walking toward her room. I couldn't help but admire her body as she all but glided down the hall. Her ass was fuller than it once was, but it looked good on her. The way her hips swayed was damn near hypnotic. Before I was ready to take my eyes off of her delectable ass, we arrived at her room.

She closed the door and turned to face me. I could see the apprehension written all over her. Shakily, she gestured to a chair in the corner of the room and slowly inched her way toward the bed.

"Wait," I said sharply. "I want to see some of the Annabelle I have wanted to see for two decades. Go take those colored contacts out."

She blinked at me. Then, blinked again. "O-okay, Phoenix." She scurried to the bathroom. I dropped into the chair, completely stunned that she didn't balk at my demand. I should have asked her, but those fucking green eyes were pissing me the fuck off. Those weren't her eyes. I wanted to see the baby blues that only two other people in the world had, our children.

She came back into the room with her eyes downcast. When she took a seat on the bed, she kept her eyes on the floor. "Look at me, Annabelle," I said softly.

She slowly raised her head and, finally, her eyes. It was like a punch to the gut. There she was.

My girl.

My love.

My Annabelle.

I stood and took two long strides to reach her. I cupped the back of her neck and pulled her to her feet. My other hand cupped her cheek as I brought my face closer to hers. "Annabelle," I breathed, "I've missed you so damn much." Then, I covered her mouth with mine. Home. I was finally fucking home.

CHAPTER SIXTEEN

Annabelle

Nothing in this world would ever compare to Phoenix's lips on mine. They were the poison and the antidote, one in the same. His kiss started soft, just a touch of his lips to mine. It quickly became more urgent. He pressed harder, squeezing me to him. When his tongue slipped into my mouth, I think my heart stopped for several beats. I melted into his embrace, kissing him back with 20 years' worth of passion.

Suddenly, he pulled his lips away from mine, but continued to cup my cheek with his hand. His eyes were wild, his breathing heavy. He groaned, "That was the hardest thing I have ever done, pulling away from you, but we need to talk first. Just, promise me one thing?"

"What?" I asked. I would promise him anything.

"Promise you'll let me kiss you again when all is said and done."

I felt myself blush like a teenager. The things this man could do to me. "I promise," I said softly, trying to mask my smile.

His hand slid from my cheek to my neck where he gently caressed my skin. "What happened to your birthmark?"

Suddenly feeling self-conscious, I took a step back and covered my neck with my hand. "I had it lasered off years ago. I was told to keep it covered because it was a distinct physical characteristic, and I got tired of covering it with makeup every morning."

Phoenix nodded in understanding. After several beats of silence, he quietly asked, "Do you still have it?"

The hand covering my neck automatically moved to my forearm and absently rubbed over the area hidden underneath my sleeve. "Yes, I do."

"Show me."

I pushed my sleeve up and held my arm out

to him. His large hand wrapped around my arm and his thumb reverently smoothed over the faint scar.

"Do you still have yours?" I asked.

One side of his mouth curved up into a half-smile as he nodded and extended his arm. There it was. The letter A lightly scarred into his skin framed by an ornate tribal tattoo.

I reached out and ran my fingers over the area, remembering the night we forever marked our bodies to show our love for each other.

I was brought back to the present when Phoenix cleared his throat and moved to take a seat on the bed. He kicked his boots off and situated himself so he was propped up against the headboard. "This is going to be a long conversation. Thought we might as well get comfortable."

I nodded in agreement and moved to sit beside him, leaning back against the headboard as well. I pulled a pillow into my lap so I would have something to fidget with. I always fidgeted when I was nervous, and nervous didn't even begin to cover how I was feeling. There were things I was going to have to tell him that I didn't want to relive. I'm sure he had things to say to me that I didn't want to hear. I decided to get the ball rolling. "How did you find me?"

"Octavius had a file containing a lot of information about you. In that file were hospital records for a Jane Doe and a Johnny Doe. It also contained handwritten notes made by Octavius. He thought you and Nivan were Jane and Johnny. Anyway, the thing that caught my eye was a doctor's name on the hospital reports. That doctor is now a member of my club. I asked him about it. He told me what he knew, and I went from there. To make a long story short, the guy that helped you, Luke, is a friend of mine."

"Kathleen's brother?" I asked.

"Yes. He's also the one who led the investigation against Octavius and his men. Ultimately, the farm and all associated property were raided, all of Octavius's men were arrested, and the entire operation was shut down," he explained.

The entire operation was shut down. That sounded too good to be true. Before he said anything else, I had to know, "Are you absolutely sure Octavius is dead?"

He reached inside his cut and pulled out some papers. Shuffling through them, he removed two pieces and handed them to me. I couldn't believe what I was holding in my hand. Octavius Jones's death certificate. It should have been wrong to feel as happy as I did seeing in official black and white that Octavius was dead. Wrong or right, I didn't care. Tears of relief freely streamed down my face. "It's over," I whispered. "It's finally over."

Phoenix shifted his weight. "He's not a threat to you anymore, but it's not over yet." I looked at him quizzically. "I'm afraid some of the things I have to tell you, things that he is responsible for, will hurt you. I damn sure know they hurt me, but once you know everything, that's when it will be over."

My body shook with silent sobs. Would I ever be able to live my life without Octavius hanging over my head? What else could there be? By threatening the love of my life and his family, he stole my life from me, held me prisoner, and made me give him a son, not to mention the other loss I solely blamed him for, my sweet, innocent baby girl.

"Hey, it's not all bad. I was upset at first, really fucking upset, but it turned out to be a good thing. Before we get to that part, let's start with something easy, yeah?" I nodded my agreement. That sounded like a great idea to me. "Okay, is Nathan really Octavius's son, Nivan?"

I choked on a sob. "Yes, but not like you think, and you can't tell him, Nathan, I mean.

He doesn't know. He was too young to remember much. He thinks his dad was a Marine who died in combat." My rambling stopped abruptly when I realized what I'd said.

Shit.

Shit.

Shit.

I had almost convinced myself that story was the truth, and it rolled off my tongue easily.

"It's okay. It doesn't matter what you told him, and he doesn't have to know if you don't want him to. I'm not here to disrupt his life. What did you mean by 'not like you think'?"

A large part of me really wanted to tell him this and another part of me was utterly embarrassed. Bracing myself for his reaction, I heaved in a breath and blurted, "Nathan is Octavius's biological son, but he wasn't conceived in the way nature intended." There, that wasn't so bad.

Phoenix cocked his head to the side. "I'm not following you, sweetheart."

"I didn't have sex with Octavius to conceive Nathan. I agreed to give him a son, I did not agree to give him myself, so Nathan was conceived by in vitro fertilization. I'm sorry, but I refuse to refer to my son by that other ridiculous name. I would appreciate it if you did the same."

Phoenix had the biggest smile on his face. "I can do that. Nathan it is."

I shook my head. "You're such a man. Unpuff your chest, you big bastard."

Phoenix threw his head back and laughed. "I won't apologize for being happy about that," he said through his laughter.

I giggled. "Yeah, I was quite proud of myself for figuring out a way around it. Octavius was a stickler for deals and agreements. He had this hang-up about being true to your word. Once I pointed out the technicality, he didn't argue with me. He only cared about having a son to inherit the—oh, is that why you're here?"

Phoenix sat up straighter. "No. That is not why I am here. I am here for you." He turned his body toward me. "You don't know what it has been like for me. I came back and you were gone. I looked everywhere for you. I've never stopped looking for you. It was like one day there was an Annabelle Burnett and the next day there wasn't. The best private investigators in the country couldn't find you. Hell, I even had Luke trying to find you."

"I can explain that. When Kathleen asked Luke to help me, he told her he didn't want to know my real name. She drove me to the hospital, and

I was admitted as Jane Doe. Your doctor friend helped me sneak out the back of the hospital where an SUV was waiting. I got in, was flown across the country, and given a new identity. Luke never knew who I was," I told him.

"You just saved him from one hell of an ass-kicking," he said, completely serious.

"What about Nathan? I have a report for a Johnny Doe saying he arrived with you and was later found dead in his hospital bed."

My eyes widened in surprise. "That must have been something Luke did to help cover our tracks. Kathleen carried Nathan into the hospital and held him in her lap like he was her son while I was admitted. Since she supposedly didn't know me, there was no reason for her to stay with me. She left the hospital with Nathan and handed him over to an agent who was waiting down the road. Once he had Nathan, he drove to the back of the hospital and waited for me to be brought out."

Phoenix nodded. "Yeah, it sounds like Luke did a pretty good job of covering your tracks. I did find a death certificate for Nivan in Octavius's files, but it's obviously fake. From what I could tell, he was never able to prove Johnny Doe was actually Nivan. Sorry, Nathan."

"So, if Octavius is dead and everyone thought Nathan died years ago, who did inherit the farm?" I asked hesitantly. I didn't think Octavius had any other living relatives, and I was suddenly afraid that he did. Would I need to hide from them for the rest of my life, too?

Phoenix's face fell, and his posture went from relaxed to rigid. He gritted out, "I did."

"What?" I shrieked, leaping off the bed.

He pinched the bridge of his nose and sighed, "I recently found out my mother was married to Octavius's father, Zayne, before she was married to the man I thought was my father. So, yeah, I'm actually Zayne's firstborn son, the rightful inheritor of the dairy farm."

"You're Octavius's brother?" I asked in disbelief.

"Half-brother biologically, but I don't claim him or anyone in that family. I am a Black through and through."

"Wait. You said the farm was raided and all operations were shut down. How did you inherit it if it was shut down?" I asked. I was so confused. It seemed like there was too much for my brain to keep up with.

"I should have said the illegal operations were shut down. The dairy farm itself was legit, but Octavius was using the land and other facilities on the property for numerous illegal activities. Gun running, drug distribution, loan sharking, kidnapping, human trafficking, the list goes on and on. I had no part in it and completely cooperated with the police during the investigation. Since I didn't even know I had rights to the property, let alone what was going on out there, the property was deemed mine once the investigation was wrapped up," he explained.

"I had no idea he was doing all of those things! I knew about the loan sharking, of course, because that's how I ended up there, but I didn't know anything about all of the other stuff." A thought suddenly occurred to me. "Oh, Phoenix, were Kathleen and her husband arrested?"

He shook his head and softly smiled. "No, they were and still are legit employees of the dairy farm."

That was good to hear. If it weren't for Kathleen, the last 13 years of my life would have been hell. She would forever hold a special place in my heart for what she did for me and my son.

A sharp knock on my door startled me. Before I could ask who it was, the door flew open revealing Token. "Taylor, we need you out front right now!" Token shouted. That could only mean one thing.

I think my feet hit the ground once between my bed and the hallway. I ran as fast as I could to the front doors, which were luckily being held open for me. Skidding to a halt in the forecourt, I found exactly what I expected to find. My son had another young man pinned to the ground.

Nathan's fury was palpable, but this wasn't my first rodeo. Walking closer to my son, I softly said, "Nathan, let him go."

His nostrils flared, and he tightened the hand around the guy's throat. "Not happening," he grunted.

I moved a step or two closer, "Let him go, sweetheart. Token will hold him while you tell us what happened."

"Not this time, Mom. This one is mine this time."

I wasn't surprised that my usual methods weren't working. Nothing about the day had been typical. Why not end it with my son killing what looked to be one of Wave's newer prospects?

"Give me one good reason why I should let you continue kicking this kid's ass," I demanded.

Nathan's face reddened even more, and I swear steam shot out of his nose. "He called you a muffler bunny and said I was nothing but a biker bastard still attached to your tit."

Out of nowhere, Phoenix's booted foot slammed into the side of the kid's head, effectively knocking him out. Nathan looked up at Phoenix, his mouth agape. "Sorry to steal your thunder, kid, but nobody talks about your mother that way and gets away with it."

"Damn straight! Strip his cut and put his punk ass on the curb!" Wave shouted, pushing his way through the crowd.

I placed my hands on Nathan's shoulders. "Come on, baby, let's go back inside and let them handle this."

He reluctantly moved off of the unconscious man-child and let me lead him inside. I guided him back to my room. Once inside, I pulled him in for a hug. He'd been bigger than me for a long time, but he was still my baby. "Are you okay, son?"

He huffed. "I'm fine. I was fine, but the little fucker just wouldn't shut up."

"Language," I admonished with a smile.

Phoenix and Wave came through the door, without knocking I might add. Nathan turned to Phoenix and held out his hand. "Thank you, sir."

Phoenix grinned. "My pleasure. Nice job taking

him down."

My sweet Nathan's cheeks flushed. Wave clapped him on the shoulder. "Our Nathan here has been working his ass off the last few years and, as of today, he is officially the newest member of the MMA team for the Northwest division of the United States Fighting League."

"No shit? Congratulations, kid! That's quite an accomplishment. I'm surprised you aren't out celebrating," Phoenix said sincerely.

"I wouldn't have made it to where I am if it weren't for my mom and the Knights. There's nowhere else I would rather be celebrating tonight," Nathan replied.

Phoenix directed his attention to me. "I'm going to head back to the hotel I'm staying at, let you and your boy celebrate your good news. We can catch up more tomorrow?"

I really, really wanted him to stay, but he was right. This was a huge moment for Nathan and I had done nothing but monopolize it. "Yes, tomorrow sounds good."

Phoenix leaned closer, his deep voice awakening every nerve ending located in an erogenous zone, "You gonna make it easy on me and give me your number or are you going to make me hunt your fine ass down again?"

I managed to sputter out my phone number when all I wanted to do was kick everyone out, throw myself on the floor, and beg him to have his wicked way with me.

Phoenix stepped closer and pulled me into a hug. Well, what I thought was going to be a hug. He turned his body so he was shielding me from the other eyes in the room. His hand slid down to cup my ass while his lips latched onto my earlobe. He growled just low enough for me to hear, "I'm coming back for you in the morning. You best be ready for me." He squeezed my ass cheek hard, placed a kiss on my temple, and left the room.

CHAPTER SEVENTEEN

Phoenix

When I got back to my hotel room, I didn't know whether to punch a hole in the wall or jack off until my dick was raw. Never before had I experienced such a mixture of emotions. One thing was certain though, I wanted Annabelle and I was going to make damn sure I had her.

I was still in the middle of my internal debate as to the best way to release some of my pent-up frustration when my phone rang, Dash's name appearing on the screen. "Dash, what's up?"

"Hey, Prez. How's your trip going?" he asked.

"Did my daughter put you up to this?"

He chuckled. "No, but I fully expected her to. Thought I would put myself one step ahead of her and call while she's asleep."

"Why is she asleep? She doesn't usually go to bed this early."

"She came home from work early today and said she didn't feel good. She went on to say she thought she was just overly exhausted and needed to get some sleep."

"If she's not feeling better in the morning, you call Patch and have him check her over, no matter what she says," I ordered.

"I'm one step ahead of you, too," he chuckled. "I already called him and asked him to stop by the house or her office tomorrow and check in on her."

"You think she's coming down with something?"

"Honestly, I think it's stress. She won't stop fussing over Coal. Now, you're gone on a solo run, and she knows that's bullshit no matter what anyone tells her. Add in everything that just went down with Reese and Duke, it's not surprising she's worrying herself sick."

"Let me know what Patch says tomorrow, yeah?" Fuck, I hoped there wasn't anything wrong with my baby girl. My plate was full,

I couldn't handle anything else, especially if that something involved one of my kids. It was a small comfort to know they were both being looked after, but I still wished I could be in both places at the same time.

"Will do, Prez. You okay, man?" he asked.

I sighed and dropped my ass to the bed. "I found her."

"Yeah? You talk to her?"

I gave him the short version of my encounter with Annabelle, leaving out any and all information about Nathan. I trusted him, but my daughter was a clever woman. If he knew something he wasn't telling her, she would pick up on it and do everything she could to find out what it was. She needed to hear about Nathan from me or her mother. Of course, that would have to be after her mother heard about her, and her brother.

I finished up with Dash and fell into bed. I tossed and turned all night. Every time I drifted off to sleep, my dreams were filled with the nightmares of my past, some real and others imagined.

CHAPTER EIGHTEEN

Annabelle

Phoenix arrived at the clubhouse around lunchtime the next day. He looked like he hardly slept. I probably looked very much the same. I don't think I slept more than two hours. I couldn't stop thinking about Phoenix and all the things I needed to tell him, and wondering what things he had to tell me.

We made small talk with Wave and Token before heading out for lunch. Nathan had already left to meet with his new team at the gym and would be gone all day. I didn't usually work on the weekends, so I had the entire day free to spend with Phoenix.

We stopped for lunch at a little cafe along

the Pacific Coast Highway. After we placed our order, I asked a question I wasn't sure I wanted to know the answer to. "How did you become the president of your great-uncle's club?"

"When Uncle Talon died of a heart attack in 2002, his son, Hawk, became the president. A few years later, Hawk and his wife, Goldie, were hit when they were out for a ride. Both were killed on impact. Copper and Bronze were too young to take over the role as president, so it was offered to me. I was already a patched member, but I wasn't around much because I was still on active duty. It just so happened that their deaths occurred around the time I was up for reenlistment. Instead of reenlisting like I had originally planned, I chose to accept the offer and became the president of Blackwings."

"So, do you live in Devil Springs or Croftridge?" I asked, completely confused.

He chuckled. "I lived in Devil Springs when I first took over the club. I was president for less than a year when Gram and Pop told me they were moving to Florida and turning over the house and property to me. After discussing it with Pop and then the club, I made the decision to move the club to Croftridge, which is where I live now."

I was afraid to ask after learning so many of his family members had died over the years, but I had to know. "Your grandparents? Are they—"

He cut me off, and I was thankful for the interruption. "They are alive and well, enjoying their retirement on the Floridian coast."

I exhaled in relief. Phoenix's grandparents had a very special place in my heart, and it would have pained me greatly to know they were no longer a part of this world.

"What about Copper and Bronze? Are they members of the club?"

"Yes, they are. They recently started their own chapter of Blackwings in Devil Springs. Copper is the president and Bronze is the VP. Their chapter is still new, but they're strong. Copper has proven himself to be an invaluable asset to the club over the last year and a half, but those are stories for a different time."

After lunch, we rode to a somewhat secluded beach. It was a little difficult to reach, but it was well worth the trek once you got there. When we reached the sand, we both kicked off our shoes. Phoenix silently took my hand and started walking along the shore. We walked a good half mile before either one of us said a word.

"As much as I'm enjoying just being with you,

we do have some important things to talk about," Phoenix said, giving my hand a gentle squeeze.

"You're right, we do," I agreed. I brought my hand to my mouth and started nibbling at my fingernail. It was a disgusting habit, but I was nervous as hell, so there was no point in trying to stop myself.

I had something huge to tell Phoenix, and I didn't know how he was going to take it. It was the main thing that kept me awake the night before. My news would be extremely painful for him to hear and for me to tell.

"This is hard for me to say," I said at the same time he asked, "Do you want to sit for this?"

I shook my head. "No, I need to keep walking to share this with you."

"Okay, let's keep going," he said, tightening his grip on my hand.

"I'm guessing you know how I ended up at the farm," I surmised.

He nodded. "Your parents."

"Right." My parents were useless beings who did nothing but destroy my life because of their own selfish needs. "Octavius had been loaning money to my parents for months, all of which they gambled away or spent on alcohol and cigarettes. A few weeks after you left for the

Marines, Octavius came to collect his money. Since they couldn't pay, he took them to the farm to start working off their debt, and I had to go with them."

"At first, it wasn't so bad. I was separated from my parents and placed in a room much nicer than anything I ever had growing up. Then, Octavius started coming around more, asking me to go on a date with him. I repeatedly told him no, but he kept asking. He started bringing gifts with him when he came to see me, nice gifts, but I refused to accept any of them. Finally, he gave up on asking and started trying to use my parents as bargaining chips, saying he would reduce the amount they owed him if I would date him." I scoffed. "He had no idea how much I loathed my parents. I finally told him I was in love with you, and there was nothing he could do to change that."

I stayed silent for a few minutes, gathering my strength for the next part of the conversation. I gradually stopped walking and turned to face the water while I spoke. "By this time, several weeks had gone by since you left. Even after I told Octavius I was in love with you and waiting for you to come back, he still kept pressuring me to give him a chance. He finally stopped asking me when I told him I was pregnant with your baby."

The tears had already started. Phoenix stood behind me, his hands on my shoulders as we both stared into the deep blue sea. I expected an outburst from Phoenix, but he remained silent behind me, so I continued. "He told me he would let me keep the baby and even provide me with prenatal care if I agreed to marry him and bear him a son. He said I could leave after I gave him a son, but I had to leave the boy with him. I refused, Phoenix. I didn't want to have his child, but he said he would have our baby aborted. I couldn't let that happen. I thought if I could get through having a son for him, I could leave with our child and go straight to the police. They would arrest Octavius, and I would have both of my children, but that's not at all what happened."

My breath hitched with a sob and I had to take a moment to compose myself. Phoenix gently turned me by my shoulders and pulled me into his chest. He held me tightly to him, one arm around my waist and the other cupping the back of my head. "She died, Phoenix!" I screamed as I beat my fist on his chest. "Our baby girl died! I did everything I could to make sure she was healthy and get us out of there, and she died!"

Phoenix took us to the ground, rocking me back and forth while I cried my pain into his chest. "I didn't even get to see her or hold her before they took her away. One picture of her, that's all I've ever had of my baby girl. I'm so sorry, Phoenix! I'm sorry I lost her!"

Phoenix stopped rocking me and tightened his arms around me. He spoke softly, his mouth right beside my ear, "There's nothing to be sorry for, doll face. Nothing at all." I cried even harder, clutching his shirt and praying he never let me go.

"I wanted her," I bawled. "I wanted her, and I wanted you. It wasn't fair!"

CHAPTER NINETEEN

Phoenix

I held Annabelle in my arms while she cried, my heart breaking as the pain she had carried for years poured from her soul. "Let it out, baby. I've got you," I promised.

How was I going to tell her that Ember was alive and well? And Coal? She hadn't mentioned a thing about Coal. Surely, she knew about him.

When she started to calm, I eased her face away from my chest so I could wipe the tears from her cheeks. Her blue eyes held so many emotions—pain, anger, fear. "Tell me what happened," I said softly.

"I-I don't really know. I went into labor one morning. I told Octavius my water broke, and he took me to see the doctor at the infirmary on the farm. He confirmed the labor and took me to one of the rooms at the very back of the clinic. He said I needed to have a C-section. He put some medicine in an IV, and the next thing I knew, I was waking up in a lot of pain and being told that my baby girl was stillborn."

She looked down at her hands. "They wouldn't let me see her. I begged and begged, but Octavius said they had already taken her away. I was furious with him, and he knew it, too. I demanded that he let me name her." Her breath hitched again, "I named her Ember Rose Blackburn. I wanted her to have a piece of me and a piece of you in her name."

I kissed her cheek and pulled her closer. "It's beautiful."

I was gearing up to tell her that Ember was still alive, happy and healthy in Croftridge when she continued, "I was a mess after that, for a long time. I fell into a depression so deep I didn't think I would ever find my way back. Through my entire pregnancy with Nathan and especially after his birth, I was in a very dark place. I did what I needed to do for him, but I built a wall around my heart, and nothing was breaking it down. I'm ashamed to say that even my newborn son couldn't make my heart feel anything. For a long time, I resented Nathan. I didn't understand why the baby I wanted didn't live, but the baby I didn't want was born healthy. I hate myself for that now."

"You obviously love Nathan very much, and I'm sure you did then, too, it was just masked by the pain of losing your firstborn. When did you finally pull through the depression?" I asked.

"It was when Nathan was around two years old. Octavius was fed up with me. He said if other people were going to take care of my child, I was going to take care of other people's children. There was a daycare on the property for the children of the workers. He sent me to work there."

"And that helped you?" I asked softly.

She gave me a small smile. "Yes, it did." She turned her face to the side, staring off into the distance, obviously remembering something from that time. "There was a little girl at the daycare. She was around the same age our daughter would have been. She was like a little angel. The first day I was there, she ran up to me and begged me to hold her. When I picked her up, she wrapped her little arms around my neck and hugged me with every ounce of her strength.

Something inside me was healed by that one hug from her. I've thought about her often over the years, and I always wondered what became of her."

I was pretty sure I knew who this little girl was, but I asked anyway, "What was her name?"

She turned her eyes back to me. "Her name was Amber, Amber Smith."

"Annabelle," I blew out a long breath, "there's something you need to know." I wasn't sure if I should hold her close when I delivered the news or give her some space. I opted for something in between and placed her on the sand beside me. Intertwining my fingers with hers, I brought her hand to my lips for a soft kiss.

Holding her hand against my chest, I began, "What I'm about to tell you is going to be hard to hear, and you're not going to believe it, but I promise, it is the truth, and I can prove it."

"Please, just tell me whatever it is," she begged.

"That little girl's name wasn't Amber. It was Ember. Our daughter is alive and living in Croftridge," I said, trying to keep my voice as even as possible. Of all the reactions I expected, I did not anticipate Annabelle jerking her hand from mine and slapping me across the face.

"You fucking bastard!" she screamed, getting to her feet. "Why would you say that? Why,

Phoenix? WHY?"

I remained seated on the sand, letting her have her moment. I calmly reached into my cut and pulled out the paternity test results. "I said it because it is the truth. Here," I said, holding the papers out for her to take.

She hesitantly took them from my hand. "What is this?"

"Those are the results of the paternity test we had done to confirm that she is my biological child," I explained.

She was already shaking her head. "That doesn't mean she is my child! My child died!"

"No, Annabelle, she didn't. Octavius took her from you. He wouldn't let you see her after she was born because she was alive. I'm guessing that's also why they put you to sleep for the C-section, so you wouldn't know she was alive when she was born."

The horror on her face was something I would never be able to erase from my mind. She was backing away from me, shaking her head, muttering, "No, no, no."

"Was Ember born on June 5, 1999, at 11:26 am?" I asked.

She dropped to her knees. "Yes!" Annabelle then folded in on herself and let out a sound of pain that chilled me to my core. She raised herself up a moment later. "Where is she? I want to see her."

I stayed put and spoke evenly, "She lives in Croftridge, and you can definitely see her. She wants to see you. She has been helping me look for you this last year, but before we get to that, there's more."

"I can't take any more, Phoenix. I just can't," she whispered between hiccupping sobs.

"I know it's hard, doll face. It was for me, too, but you need to know."

"Fine. Spit it out," she spat. Good, a little anger would help her handle the next bombshell.

"When you delivered Ember, you also delivered a healthy baby boy. Octavius didn't tell you and had him raised right under your nose, just like he did with Ember," I said and handed her the next set of papers.

She snatched them from my hand, glanced over them, and screamed her fury to the sky. She whirled around, clutching those papers in her hand. "Coal Martin is my son? Did Kathleen know about this?"

"No, she didn't know he was your son. She does now, but she had no idea then. She didn't know about Ember either."

"How did you find out about all of this?" she asked.

I sighed. "It's a complicated story, that I will gladly share with you sometime, but I don't think now is the time for it."

"Why not? You've already sliced me open. Why not keep going?" she snarled.

"Annabelle, I didn't tell you about the twins to hurt you. You had a right to know. Would you have rather not known about them?" I asked.

She heaved in breath after breath. "No. Yes. I mean, they're my children, of course, I want to know about them. I want to see them. It's just a lot to process and you're telling me there's more. I can't go through this again. I would rather hear whatever it is now."

I got to my feet and approached her. I bent down and pulled her into my arms. "That was the worst of it, doll face. Everything else is just details."

We stayed on the beach a little while longer, just holding each other. I hated what she was going through. I remembered it all too well when I found out about Ember and, not that long ago, Coal. She quietly cried off and on, lost in her own thoughts. Eventually, she asked me to take her home, and reluctantly, I did.

CHAPTER TWENTY

Annabelle

Phoenix dropped me off at my house just before dark. I should have invited him in, but I needed some time alone. I think he did, too. He kissed me on the cheek and asked if he could come over in the morning. I said that would be fine, and after a quick hug, he left.

It was odd for me to be home alone on a Saturday night. I was usually at the clubhouse or at one of Nathan's matches. As much as I didn't want to, I needed to use the time alone to process everything Phoenix had shared with me.

Grabbing a bottle of wine, I opened it and headed straight to my bathroom. A nice hot bath and a bottle of wine were the comforts I rarely had time for but desperately needed. I sank into the sudsy water, laid my head back, and closed my eyes.

So many emotions were coursing through me, but two were the most prominent. Guilt and shame. How could I have been pregnant with two babies and not known? How could I have looked at my own child every day for years and not recognized her? How could I have looked at Coal several times a week and not recognized him? How could I have taken Nathan away and left the two of them there under Octavius's rule?

They probably hated me. Who could blame them? I hated my parents, and they had done far less to me than I did to my own children. What could I even say to them? "I'm sorry, your mother is the stupidest woman alive. I brought you into this world, but I'm such an idiot I couldn't even recognize my own children." I deserved for them to hate me.

And Nathan. What was I going to do about Nathan? He had a right to know about his siblings and they had a right to know about him, but that meant telling him things I had kept hidden from him all these years. When he found out what I had done, he would hate me, too. I was going to lose everyone, and it was no one's fault but my own.

I had no choice but to face the music. I would tell Nathan the truth about our past. I would go to Croftridge and see my children and own up to the mistakes I made. Then, I would leave. They would all be better off without me.

With my decision made, I finished off the bottle of wine and climbed out of the tub. I didn't bother with my usual bedtime routine, didn't even run a comb through my hair. I slipped on a t-shirt and a pair of yoga pants. Then, I crawled into bed and cried myself to sleep.

When Phoenix arrived the next morning, I had already been awake for several hours. He followed me into the kitchen and took a seat at the table. "Nathan is still sleeping. I haven't figured out how to go about telling him about Ember and Coal, not to mention everything else I've kept from him. I would appreciate it if we could hold off on discussing anything of that nature until after he is gone for the rest of the day."

"That's not a problem, Annabelle," he replied.

"On that note, can you call me Taylor in front of him, at least for now?" I asked. If Nathan heard Phoenix calling me Annabelle, it would raise questions I was not ready to answer.

Phoenix's lips pressed into a hard line. "I'll try."

We made small talk for the next hour. Surprisingly, it wasn't uncomfortable at all. It felt like old times, when we were teenagers. There had always been a natural ease between me and Phoenix, and I was relieved to know it was still there.

I was in the middle of telling Phoenix about my job at the tattoo shop when Nathan walked into the kitchen. "Morning, sweetheart," I said. I gestured across the table. "You remember Phoenix?"

Nathan nodded. "Yes. Good morning, sir." He redirected his attention to me. "I have to meet the team at the gym to go over some things before we start training tomorrow." He lowered his voice, "Are you okay with him being here?"

I placed my hand on my son's arm. "I'm fine, honey. No need for you to worry."

He leaned down to give me a hug and a kiss. "I should be home around 8:00 pm. I love you."

"I love you, too." He gave Phoenix a stern look before he turned and walked out the front door.

"He sure is protective of you," Phoenix said with a smile.

"Yeah, he is. It was just the two of us for a long

time. He didn't realize it when he was younger, but when he got older, it was obvious to him that I was being protected from something by the Knights. He never said anything about it, he just started mimicking their behavior," I explained.

"He seems like a good kid."

I smiled. "Thank you. He really is. I'm so proud of him, landing that MMA contract. He's worked hard for it. Wave and some of his members helped him with his training when he first started."

"Will he stay here while he's training?" Phoenix asked.

"Yes, he will be here most of the time. He has to go to L.A. for a six-week training camp that starts tomorrow. Then, he will be home until the scheduled fights start. The team travels as a unit, so even if he isn't slated to fight, he still has to be there."

"Would you be willing to come to Croftridge while he is away training?" he asked.

His question caught me off guard. "When?"

"I have to head back home soon. You can come with me if you want," he said.

He was asking me to ride across the country on the back of his bike. Just the two of us. I had fantasized about the two of us taking off on his bike countless times over the last 20 years. Even last week I would have given my right kidney for that fantasy to become a reality, but things had changed, drastically. I wouldn't be riding off into the sunset with Phoenix. I would be riding to a life I left behind, to children I left behind.

"I would have to talk to my boss. I don't know that I can take that much time off work with such short notice. When are you planning on leaving?"

"That depends. If you'll go with me, I would like to leave tomorrow. If not, I'll probably head out Tuesday. I gotta tell you, Annabelle, I damn sure don't want to leave you here. I want you with me, where you were always meant to be."

Before my brain realized what I was saying, the words were out of my mouth, "Let me talk to Wave about work. I'll be right back."

I excused myself from the table and went into my bedroom to make the call. I didn't want to go to Croftridge as much as I did want to go. I hurriedly dialed Wave. "Half pint! What's up?"

"Hey, Wave. Um, I need to talk to you about work," I said.

"All right. What is it?"

"Would it be possible for me to take some time off?"

"How much time and when?" he asked.

138

"That's the thing...I don't know how much time, but it would start tomorrow." I braced myself for his reaction.

He cleared his throat. "What's going on, Taylor? Is everything okay?"

"Yes and no. I'm fine, but after talking with Phoenix, I need to go back to Croftridge. I'm going to have to go back there one way or another, but he's leaving tomorrow and offered me a ride. It's not a big deal. I can always fly out there later on," I rambled.

"Half pint, do you want to go with him?"

"I think I do," I almost whispered.

"Listen here, you go with him, and you can take as much time as you need on one condition."

"And that is?" I asked.

"You have to check in with me every couple of days."

I smiled. "I can do that."

"Does Nathan know you're going back with him?" he asked carefully.

"No, he doesn't, and I would like to keep it that way. I need to feel things out in Croftridge before I talk to Nathan."

"All right. If you need anything, and I mean anything, you call me or Token. I don't care if you're here or half-way across the country, we'll come get you."

"Thanks, Wave. You guys are the best. Love you."

"Love you, too, half pint. Be safe."

I sat there for a while after the call disconnected. What had I gotten myself into? I wanted to go with Phoenix. A ride across the country with him was literally my dream come true. It was everything else that terrified me. How was I going to face the children I left behind?

The sound of my bedroom door creaking open had my head shooting up to see Phoenix filling the doorway, his hands braced on the top of the door frame. "You've been in here for a while. You okay?"

I cleared my throat and licked my dry lips. "Yeah. I was able to get the time off from work. I can leave with you tomorrow."

"You don't seem so happy about that," he observed, taking a few steps closer.

"I'm not happy about it. I'm terrified," I whispered as tears began to fall from my eyes.

He sat down on the bed beside me and put his arm around my shoulder. "There's no reason to be scared. Octavius can't hurt you or anyone else anymore."

"It doesn't have anything to do with him."

"Ah, you're worried about seeing Ember and Coal." I nodded even though it wasn't a question. "They are going to be ecstatic when I roll into town with you in tow. They don't know where I went or why I left last week, but they both know that I have been looking for you. I already told you Ember was helping me try to find you. Coal would have helped, too, but he only recently found out about you and me being his biological parents. And, he's had some other things going on that have kept him from diving into the search head first."

"They don't hate me?" I asked.

"Why on earth would they hate you, Annabelle?"

"Because I left them behind," I wailed, my head falling against his chest.

He closed both arms around me and held me while I cried all over him yet again. "You didn't leave them behind intentionally. You thought Ember was dead. She even thought you were dead. We both did until about a year ago and even then we weren't sure if you were alive or not. As for Coal, you didn't even know about him. I haven't kept the truth from them, Annabelle. They know exactly what happened."

"What kind of mother doesn't recognize her

own children? I saw Ember almost every day for years, and I saw Coal several times a week," I cried.

"Let me ask you something. When you hear about babies getting switched at birth, do you blame the mothers for not realizing the baby they took home wasn't their biological child?"

"Of course not," I replied indignantly.

"Ember and Coal ran into each other a few times on the farm. Do you blame them for not recognizing their own twin?"

"Again, of course not!"

"Then why are you beating yourself up for the same thing? They don't blame you and neither do I, because none of that was your fault," he said with so much vehemence I almost believed him. "It was a fucked up thing that happened to our family, but what's done is done, and we can't go back and change it. Only thing we can do is move forward."

I sat up and wiped the tears from my eyes. "You're right. I know you're right." I clapped my hands together loudly and stood. "I guess I need to get myself packed and ready to go back to Croftridge."

He saw right through my façade. He had always been able to read me better than anyone else, and apparently, that hadn't changed. He got to his feet and kissed my forehead. "It'll be okay, doll face, I promise."

I hoped he was right.

CHAPTER TWENTY-ONE

Phoenix

When I arrived at Annabelle's house the next morning, she was waiting on her front porch, packed and ready to go. Obviously, she had spent a great deal of time with Wave's club over the years and had traveled with them because she had all of her things packed in a small leather duffel bag and a leather backpack. I tried not to dwell on the thought of her on the back of another man's bike.

Instead, I focused on her. She was a breathtaking sight, standing there in her tight jeans, a long-sleeved t-shirt, riding boots, and leather vest. Her long hair hung in a braid down her back. She watched me ogle her body, and

I didn't give the first fuck that she knew I was checking her out.

"Are you about done? I'd like to get on the road sometime this week," she said with a smirk.

"Oh, doll face," I groaned, "I'll never be done staring at your gorgeous body." I reached down and readjusted my cock for good measure.

She rolled her eyes and sauntered past me, shoving her duffel bag into my chest as she went by. She climbed her fine ass on the bike, slid her helmet on, and motioned for me to hurry up.

I quickly strapped her bag down and made sure everything else was secure. We synced our Bluetooth devices and started on the long journey back to Croftridge.

Even though we were synced up, we didn't talk much for the first few hours of the trip. After we stopped for lunch, Annabelle seemed to perk up a little. Finally, she asked me how I found out about Ember and Coal. Deciding it would be best to tell it like it happened, I started from the beginning, the day Ember walked into my clubhouse asking for help. By the time I finished that tale, it was time to stop for dinner.

We ate at a kitschy roadside diner and refueled at the station next door. I offered to stop for the night and find a hotel nearby, but she insisted that she was fine to ride for a few more hours. I was happy to hear that because, as it was, it was going to take us at least four days to get back home and that wasn't accounting for possible weather or traffic delays.

We rode until we reached Salt Lake City, talking off and on about the kids. During the moments of silence, I had time to think about how I wanted our journey to go. If it was just me, I would have stopped at the cheapest motel I could find for the night, but I didn't want to do that with Annabelle. This was a chance I never thought I would have with her, and I wasn't going to waste one second of it.

I pulled into the parking lot of a high-rise hotel right in the heart of the city. Annabelle gasped, "Phoenix, we can't stay here!"

"Why the hell not?" I asked.

"It's too extravagant. We just need a place to shower and sleep for the night. I'm sure there's a basic hotel around here somewhere," she rambled.

"Doll face, I want to stay here. That okay with you?"

She opened her mouth and then closed it. She did that two more times before I finally took pity on her. "How about we share a room to save on the cost? Will that make you feel better?"

Her eyes widened in surprise. "Um, yes, I guess that would be okay," she sputtered.

I kept my face neutral but I was smiling from ear to ear on the inside. The first part of my plan worked beautifully. I walked into the hotel lobby with my proverbial fingers crossed that the second part of my plan would work.

Annabelle walked over to the fountain in the middle of the lobby while I got us a room. I placed some cash on the counter and told the girl it was hers if she promised to confirm that they only had rooms with one bed available should she be asked by the beautiful woman standing in front of the fountain. She readily agreed, and that was how I got Annabelle into a hotel room with only one bed for the two of us.

As expected, Annabelle balked at the idea at first, but I convinced her that it was late, and we both needed to get some rest. We had several days of riding ahead of us, and neither one of us could afford to be tired. Reluctantly, she agreed and followed me up to the room.

She showered first. I was surprised at how little time she took in the bathroom, especially after riding all day. I just assumed she would want to soak in the bath or whatever girls did that took so damn long in there, but she was in and out in about 10 minutes. She walked out in a tiny little t-shirt and yoga pants that molded perfectly to her tight ass. I about swallowed my damn tongue when I laid eyes on her.

Once in the shower, I knew I had to take care of something or it was going to be a long painful night for me. My cock had been half hard all damn day with her snuggled up behind me, her full tits pressed against my back, but seeing her in that get up she called pajamas sent every drop of blood I had rushing to my dick. I braced one hand against the wall and wrapped the other around my throbbing cock. Gripping myself firmly, I slid my hand back and forth while I imagined the things I would do to Annabelle's firm little body if she would give me the chance. Closing my eyes, I pictured her on her knees in front of me, taking me into her mouth while she had one hand on her tits and one hand between her legs. It took about five seconds of that image before I was spurting all over the shower wall.

I finished up in the shower and realized I'd forgotten to bring my clothes with me in my rush to get away from her and her fuck me pajamas. Oh well, two could play her game. I walked back into the room with nothing but a towel around my waist.

She was sitting on the bed, and she froze when she saw me. Her cheeks flushed, and her plump lips parted. She didn't say a word, but she took her time looking at my body. I smirked. "Are you about done? I'd like to get in the bed sometime this week."

She shook her head. "Oh, Phoenix, I'll never be done staring at your gorgeous body."

I stepped closer to her. "Is that right?"

"Mmm-hmm," she replied, licking her lips.

"If you don't want this, you better get your ass in the bed and under those covers. I've been waiting almost 20 years to fuck you again, doll face, and my self-restraint is damn near tapped out," I growled.

"I-I-I," she stammered.

I slid a pair of boxer briefs on under my towel and barked, "Get in the damn bed, Annabelle."

She jolted out of her stupor and climbed under the covers faster than a child hiding from the monster under their bed. I couldn't help but chuckle.

Climbing in the bed with her, I turned off the lights and pulled her to me. I placed a kiss on the side of her face and told her, "Good night, doll face."

CHAPTER TWENTY-TWO

Phoenix

I woke Annabelle up early the next morning. I wanted to get on the road as soon as possible because I had plans for the evening, and I didn't want to take a chance of missing them. We had breakfast at the hotel, and then we were on the road by 8:00 am.

I was the happiest man in the world. The love of my life was on the back of my bike riding across the country with me. The scenery was almost as stunning as she was, and thus far, the weather had been nothing short of perfect. Annabelle seemed to be more relaxed, which only heightened my mood.

We had been on the road for about 30 minutes

when she asked, "Will you tell me how you found out about Coal?"

The next several hours were spent telling her the story of Coal. I even pointed out that he prospected for me almost a year and I had no idea he was my son. She didn't seem affected by my statement, but I hoped she would let it sink in when she had some time to herself. I debated whether or not to tell her about his injuries while we were still on the road. I guess I was silent too long, and she picked up on my unease.

"What aren't you telling me?" she asked.

I sighed. "Nothing that I planned to keep from you. I was just trying to decide if I should tell you now or wait until we've stopped for lunch. I don't want you falling off the bike," I said.

She gasped. "It's that bad?"

I reached back and patted her thigh. "It might sound that way at first, but you have to keep in mind that he is okay now. You think you can handle that?"

I heard her swallow and then her soft, "Yes, I can."

I crossed my fingers and began telling her how Coal was injured. She tensed at certain parts, but she quietly listened while I spoke. When I told her he had been shot three times, she wrapped her arms around my waist and buried her helmeted head in my back as she cried. I wanted nothing more than to pull over and take her into my arms to comfort her, but I kept going.

"It was Ember that put everything together and figured out he was her twin. He needed blood, a lot of blood, and he has a rare type. All of the brothers were getting tested, but only I was a match. They were refusing to let me donate because I had been shot, too, even though it was really just a graze. Ember overheard me arguing with the doctor. She knew that we had the same blood type so she rushed off to get tested. The nurse commented how odd it was that they had the same blood type, were the same age, and had the same birthday. As soon as she was finished donating, she told me what the nurse said. I had my tech guy dig up Coal's birth records, and you were listed as his mother. He was born two minutes after Ember. Still, I wanted to be absolutely sure, so I got Patch to run a paternity test under the radar while he was in the hospital. When we got the results, we kept things quiet until Coal was out of the woods. I wanted him to know, and I was going to tell him one way or the other, but I thought talking to Kathleen and her husband first was the right thing to do. I sat down with both of them and broke the news as gently as I could. I thanked them for raising my boy and promised them I had no intention of trying to replace them or keep them out of Coal's life. After that, we agreed to wait until he was discharged from the hospital to tell him he had some new family members. All in all, he took the news well. He already knew he was adopted, but my promise to not disrupt his relationship with Kathleen and Jeff was what put him at ease."

"When did this happen?" she asked.

I cleared my throat and braced for her reaction. "About three weeks ago."

"What?" she shrieked.

"About three weeks ago," I repeated. "I've wanted nothing more than to find you, but I wouldn't have left Croftridge if his recovery wasn't going well."

"So, he's okay?" she asked.

"He's still healing, but yeah, he's doing okay. He came home from the hospital before I left. Kathleen and Jeff still work at the dairy farm and live on the property. Ember and Dash live out there now, too, so he's got his adoptive parents and his twin sister fussing over him, not to mention the club members. He risked his life for the brothers; not a one of us will ever forget that. I promise, he's being looked after by more than enough."

I felt her nod, but she remained quiet for a few minutes, likely absorbing everything I had just shared. "Did you say Ember lives on the farm property?" she asked, her voice full of disbelief.

"Yeah, she does. Let's stop for lunch, refuel and recharge, and I will tell you what she's done with the place since I inherited it."

***

We rolled into downtown Denver around 5:00 pm. I drove straight to the hotel I picked the day before. It was another upscale hotel, but this one wasn't a large commercial chain. It had an old-world feel to it. I was looking forward to our stay because I made sure we had time to enjoy some of the amenities offered.

Annabelle didn't make a fuss about the hotel or the fact that we were sharing a room together. I didn't know if that was because she was okay with it or because she was too tired and too overwhelmed to care. Once we were checked in and settled into our room, I suggested we order room service for dinner. We took turns showering while waiting for dinner to arrive.

I couldn't have asked for anything better. They wheeled in dinner for two on one of those silver carts, complete with a bouquet of flowers and lit candles for the centerpiece. When the attendant left, I popped the cork on the champagne and poured a glass for each of us.

"What's all this?" she asked.

I tried to appear indifferent. "It's dinner. What's it look like?"

She rolled her eyes. "Phoenix, do you honestly expect me to believe that staying in these kinds of hotels and ordering romantic dinners are things you normally do when you're on the road?"

I shrugged. "I like to travel in style. What's wrong with that?"

She looked at me like I had completely lost my mind for one long second before she threw her head back and laughed. "Travel in style," she guffawed and slapped her leg. "That's priceless."

"Shut up and drink your champagne, brat," I barked.

She wiggled her fingers at me, taunting me. "Oooh, don't get all pissy with me, you stylish biker man."

She was going to pay for that, but it would have to be later, when I could enjoy making her pay. I stabbed my finger toward her plate. "Eat, woman."

She held her hands up in surrender. "Fine. You win."

We enjoyed our meal together, managing to keep the conversation light. When we finished off the bottle of champagne, I offered to send for a second bottle, but Annabelle declined. I opened the door to wheel the food cart into the hallway, surprised to find our next appointment standing there poised to knock. "Good evening, Mr. Black. Let me take care of that for you, and then we'll get set up."

Annabelle was doing her best to see who was at the door while trying to hide her interest. Good, I wanted her curiosity piqued. I stepped to the side and held the door open for our two guests and their equipment. "What's all this?" she asked, a hint of excitement in her voice.

I winked. "Thought you might enjoy a massage after two days on the back of my bike."

She smiled brightly. "Oh, that sounds absolutely wonderful."

She stiffened slightly when she realized two things: one, we would both be naked beneath a small towel for the massage and two, the hot blonde would be massaging me. She went into the bathroom to disrobe and came out completely covered in the complimentary robe provided by the hotel. She then made me promise to either close my eyes or keep them averted while she was having her back massaged. I gave her my word, but she was going to explain that to me later.

As for the hot blonde, I didn't plan it that way; it's just how it happened. Her little nose wrinkled when Svetlana introduced herself as my masseuse and led me by hand to the massage table. I swear Annabelle snarled when Svetlana cooed, "Oh, Mr. Black, you have such large muscles. It is such a treat for me to work on someone as toned as you are."

When our massages were finished, I felt great. Svetlana did an excellent job and remained very professional while she had her hands on me. Annabelle, however, was wound tighter than an eight-day clock. She hopped off her table and bolted for the bathroom. I thanked the girls, gave them both a generous tip, and walked them to the door.

Sliding on a pair of basketball shorts, I made purposeful strides to the bathroom door and gave it three sharp knocks. "Annabelle, get your ass out here right now."

"Leave me alone, Phoenix."

"I don't think so, doll face. Either you come out, or I'm coming in," I informed her.

I heard her huff and then the door swung open. She stomped toward the bed and sat down with a plop.

"What in the hell is the matter with you?" I asked.

"Oh, I don't know, Mr. Black. Your big muscles have me all tongue-tied. Here, let me just rub my big fake tits all over you and see if that helps," she said, mimicking Svetlana's voice while thrusting her chest out and shaking her tits at me.

"You're jealous, I got that, but what was with fleeing to the bathroom and making me promise not to look at you? What are you hiding from me?" I asked. Her jealousy was flattering, but I knew she was using it as a distraction, and I did not care for it one bit.

When she didn't answer me, I had to remind myself to keep my temper in check. "You *are* hiding something from me." It had to be something on her back. My control slipped, and my anger roared to life when it occurred to me that Octavius may have hurt her, and she was hiding scars from me. I balled my fists and took determined steps toward her.

Her face paled, and she started scooting backward on the bed. She pressed her back against the headboard so hard I heard the bed creak. Enough of this crap. "Show me!" I demanded.

She shook her head and pressed herself even harder against the headboard.

"Show me!" I roared and got the exact same response. I grabbed her ankles, yanked her to me, and flipped her over on her stomach before she could even make a sound. Grabbing the hem of her t-shirt, I ripped it up her back, causing a squeak to escape her. When I saw what she was hiding from me, it was like a punch to the gut. The air left my lungs. Emotions clogged my throat. I couldn't do anything but stare.

I placed my hand on her back and lightly traced the outline of the phoenix tattoo covering her entire back. The same phoenix she gave me for Christmas all those years ago. The same one that was hanging on the wall in my bedroom. It was an incredible piece of art.

I continued to softly trace the lines inked into her skin and quietly asked, "Why were you hiding this from me? It's beautiful, Annabelle."

She sniffled. "I was embarrassed. I didn't want you to think I was obsessed with you like some crazy stalker."

"Baby," I breathed as I leaned forward and began peppering her back with soft kisses. "I want you to be obsessed with me, just like I am with you."

I climbed onto the bed and kissed my way up her back, pushing her shirt up as I went. "Take this off for me." Surprisingly, she complied. I sat back on my heels, her legs extended between mine, and took in the unencumbered view of her tribute to me.

"I have one for you, too," I told her. Hers was beautiful, mine was not. Even though it was the result of a drunken dare from some of the guys on base, it was still a heartfelt gesture. As I got older, I could see how she might not find it as flattering as I originally intended it to be.

"Let me see it," she said, flipping over onto her back, showing me her succulent bare tits for the first time in almost two decades. They were bigger than before, but they were just as firm and perky as they were when she was 18 years old. Her hard nipples seemed to be pointing directly at my mouth.

I placed both hands on her waist and started slowly sliding them up her body. "Annabelle," I rasped, my eyes fixated on her chest. She looked down and gasped when she realized what she'd done. She moved to cover herself, but I caught her arms and shook my head. "No, baby, don't hide from me. Let me look at the sweet tits I've missed so much."

"Phoenix," she whined.

"I'm done holding back, Annabelle. Yeah, we got a lot of shit to work through, but I've craved you for 20 years. Twenty fucking years. Nothing will ever make me not want you. You tell me you don't want me, I'll get up and walk away, but if you say you do want me, know this, I'm fucking you until the sun comes up. What's it going to be, doll face?"

She smirked. "I want to see the tattoo first."

She had me so worked up I didn't even hesitate. I pushed my shorts down far enough for my hard cock to spring free and thrust my hips toward her face. "There it is," I growled.

Her mouth dropped open while she stared at her name tattooed down the side of my cock, my very hard, throbbing cock. She reached her hand out like she was going to touch it, the tattoo that is, and then she seemed to realize what else she would be touching and pulled her hand back. "Wh-why did you do that?" she asked.

"Because you own it. It seemed appropriate to

put your name on it," I answered immediately.

Her face crumpled and tears started sliding down the side of her face. That wasn't the reaction I wanted her to have while my erection was straining toward her lips like a heat-seeking missile. She pushed herself up and grabbed me by my shoulders, pulling me down on top of her. "I've missed you so fucking much," she groaned right before she crushed her lips to mine.

There was no way I could be gentle. I had a lot of pent up sexual tension, amongst other things, that needed an outlet. I pulled back from her, lifted her by her waist, and tossed her farther up the bed. She let out a squeal when she bounced on the mattress. I roughly slipped my fingers under the waistband of her shorts and panties and ripped them from her body.

Annabelle's naked body at 37 was the stuff fantasies were made of. Her tits were full and perfectly round, topped with rose-colored nipples. Despite having carried twins and having a third child, her stomach was flat and held very little evidence of her pregnancies, only a few stretch marks and a C-section scar. Her hips flared to give her a tantalizing hourglass shape leading my eyes right to her beautiful, bare pussy. I pushed her legs apart and growled, "Look how wet you are for me."

"Phoenix, please," she whined.

I slid my hand up her thigh and ran my finger over her slit from top to bottom. Gathering her juices on my finger, I brought it to my lips and sucked. "Mmmm," I groaned. I reached for her core again, this time slipping one finger inside her. She moaned and wriggled, but I froze. She was tight, like way too tight for a woman her age with three children.

She leaned up on her elbows, panting, "Phoenix? Is something wrong?"

I had no idea what to say. I didn't want to ask her when she was last fucked. I didn't want to know anything about her sexual experiences that weren't with me, but if I didn't say something, I was going to hurt her, and I did not want to do that. I remembered the pain on her face and the tears in her eyes when I took her virginity. It nearly killed me that night, and I had no intention of experiencing it again. Choosing my words carefully, I said, "Baby, I'm afraid I'll hurt you."

She blushed from head to toe and turned her face away from me. I crooked my finger that was still inside of her, making her gasp. "If I've got my finger in your pussy, you can damn well look at me."

She turned her head so her eyes met mine. "I'll be okay, Phoenix."

"I'm not trying to be an asshole here, but how is this even possible? You're as tight as you were when I took you for the first time," I blurted before my brain could phrase it in a less offensive way.

She narrowed her eyes and shocked the ever-loving shit out of me with her next words. "It's possible because the night you took my virginity was the last time I've had sex. My children were born via C-section, so nothing other than a tampon, my finger, or a small vibrator has been in or out of there!"

Those words from her lips were the death of my control. She was mine and always had been. I was overcome with a primal need to reclaim what was mine. I fell on top of her, thrusting my tongue into her mouth while my finger pumped in and out of her at the same tempo. I carefully added a second finger, scissoring them as I pumped in and out.

I moved my lips down her neck, down her chest, until I reached her hard, pink nipple. Sucking it into my mouth with fervor, I pulled hard on the taut bud and gently nipped it with my teeth. She clawed at my back, pulled at my hair, and moaned loud enough to let anyone in the rooms beside us know exactly what we were doing.

I switched to her other nipple to give it the same attention while I slipped a third finger inside her. I felt her tense for just a second, and then she was back to writhing and wiggling beneath me.

Dragging my mouth down her body, I didn't stop until I reached her core. Her taste filled my mouth and drove me into a frenzy. I sucked her clit and pumped my fingers furiously into her. "Come, Annabelle, fucking come," I barked.

I felt her body tense and then she was coming all over my face and hands, screaming my name loud enough for all of Denver to hear.

I couldn't take it anymore. In a flash, I moved over her and positioned myself at her entrance, ready to slide inside when a moment of clarity broke through the lust that had taken over my brain.

"Do I need to use a condom?" I asked through gritted teeth as my dick screamed at me to move forward.

At her hesitation, I added, "I'm clean. I was tested last month."

"Okay," she whispered.

"I need more than that, doll face."

Instead of answering me with her words, she pulled me forward by my ass as she raised her hips to meet me, causing me to slide inside, all the way to the hilt. My eyes damn near crossed when her tight heat engulfed me, her pussy still fluttering with the remnants of her climax.

I lost all control of myself. I pounded into her with everything I had. She was squealing and screaming, and I prayed they were sounds of bliss because it would kill me if I was hurting her.

"Phoenix, oh, oh, I'm coming! I'm coming again!" she shouted.

Damn right she was. I thrust into her hard two more times, and then I came so hard it stole my vision.

Panting, sweating, and feeling better than I had in years, I looked down at the treasure beneath me. She was just as sweaty and out of breath as I was, and thank the stars she was smiling brightly at me. "Better rehydrate, big boy, you promised to fuck me until sunrise."

I threw my head back and laughed at the little minx. "Indeed I did, doll face."

CHAPTER TWENTY-THREE

Annabelle

Phoenix softly kissed me before sliding out of my body and walking to the bathroom. He returned moments later with a washcloth and proceeded to clean me.

"I could have done that," I said, feeling slightly uncomfortable.

"I know, but I wanted to." He finished his self-appointed task and climbed into bed beside me.

My mind wandered to what Phoenix said about being tested recently. I knew it wasn't realistic to believe he had been celibate while we were apart, but it didn't make it hurt any less to have it confirmed. Were there many women? Were they just flings or did he actually have relationships with them?

"So, you're okay with not using condoms?" Phoenix asked, interrupting my mental trip down the rabbit hole.

"Uh, yeah, it's fine," I answered, trying to force my mind to stay in the present and not his unknown past.

"I haven't noticed any kind of birth control. Aren't you worried about getting pregnant?" he asked.

Still somewhat distracted by thoughts of him having experiences with other women, I answered, "No, I'm not worried about getting pregnant. I had my tubes tied not long after I left Croftridge."

Suddenly hovering over me with his nose touching mine, he growled, "You did what?"

"I had my tubes tied so I wouldn't get pregnant again," I explained.

"Why would you do something like that?" he yelled, moving off of me and walking toward the window.

"Because I wasn't going to let another man force me to have his child! Why do you care?" I yelled back. I had every right to have my tubes tied, and I wasn't about to let him make me feel bad for it.

"What if I wanted to have more children with you?"

"What?" I shrieked, my voice a good octave higher than normal. "Are you fucking insane? More children? We've spent a few days together after being apart for so many years. Yes, we had sex, but we're not even together like that," I said, gesturing between the two of us. "And if that's not a good enough reason for you, I'm too old, and I don't want any more kids." I crossed my arms and dared him to challenge me.

And challenge me he did. "Oh, doll face," he sneered, "don't lie to me. You remember what happens when you lie to me, don't you?" I refused to acknowledge his question. Yes, I remembered what happened the two times I told a little fib to him, but that was a different time under different circumstances. I wasn't going to let him distract me with thoughts of his hand on my ass.

"Keep testing me, Annabelle, you know how hard that makes me," he said, slowly advancing on me. "Let's get a few things straight right now. You're not too old, and I think you would like to have more kids, my kids. But, most importantly, we damn sure are together like that."

He closed the remaining distance between us in three quick strides. Tipping my chin up with his finger, he stared into my eyes as he whispered harshly, "Don't you dare say different." Without giving me a chance to say different, he smashed his mouth to mine in a punishing kiss. He poured all of his emotions into that kiss, and I drank them down.

Ripping his mouth from mine, he roughly flipped me onto my stomach. With a slap to my ass, he ordered, "Up on your knees."

I slid my knees under me and pushed up with my hands, only for Phoenix to plant his big palm between my shoulder blades and push me back down. He slapped a hand to my ass and kneaded my cheek while growling, "I fucking love this ass." He gave my ass one more slap before he thrust into me.

Holding onto my hips tightly, he worked himself in and out of me, hitting all the places that had been grossly neglected over the last two decades. He was so deep it was just shy of being painful, but there was no way he would be getting any complaints from me.

As if he'd read my thoughts, he fisted my hair and pulled me so that my back was against his chest. I reached up and back to cup his head with one hand while the other was braced on his large thigh. Releasing my hair, his hands moved down to hold me against his chest by my breasts.

Pinching and pulling at my nipples, he built me up higher and higher with every touch from his skilled fingers and his rhythmic thrusts. I could feel my body tighten, preparing for my release, and I knew he could feel it, too. One hand slowly trailed from my breast to the apex of my thighs. He rubbed my clit in firm circles, matching the pace of his thrusts. When the tension built to an all-time high, a strangled sound escaped my lips as I exploded in the arms of the only man to ever hold my heart.

Turning my head, I greedily took his mouth while my body continued to ripple with pleasure. While I was coming down, he found his release, groaning into my mouth as he did.

"Phoenix," I whispered against his lips.

"My Annabelle," he whispered back, gently caressing my face.

We didn't need words right then. We both knew how we felt about each other, how we'd always felt about each other. Our bodies conveyed our feelings far better than any words could.

He was true to his word and fucked me until sunrise, each time just as passionate and intense. He finally let me fall asleep in the early hours of the morning and woke me about four hours later. I had no idea how we were going to manage a full day of riding with only a few hours of sleep. It's not like I could offer to drive for him. Well, I could—Token taught me how to ride a motorcycle years ago—but Phoenix riding on the back of his own bike was as likely as finding tits on a bull.

"Are you sure you're okay to ride? I can go down and arrange a late check out so you can sleep for a few more hours," I offered.

"Woman, I've already told you, I'm fine. Now quit nagging me and let's go," he grumbled. I wasn't sure if he was joking or if he was really irritated with me, but I was leaning toward the latter. I kept my mouth shut, not wanting to irritate him further, and followed him to the bike.

We had been on the road for a little over an hour when we came upon the first construction zone. Traffic was backed up and moving at a snail's pace. Normally, this wouldn't have bothered me very much, but it was the middle of summer, and I was in riding gear. In other words, I was fucking hot. I was contemplating stripping down to a tank top when we started moving again. We were only delayed about 30 minutes, but I could tell it did nothing for Phoenix's mood.

Three more construction delays and one

major car accident had Phoenix exiting the highway and taking an alternative route. We stopped for lunch and fuel before continuing our journey on a country highway. Phoenix had been relatively quiet the entire day, but he did hold my hand to and from the diner, and he gave me an inappropriate for the public kiss after he filled his gas tank. Just those few little displays of affection gave me more comfort than I cared to admit. He was probably just tired, and I was overreacting.

Feeling a bit better, I took the time to take in the scenery. I had never been through this part of the country. While I didn't think I would like living in the Midwest, I was thoroughly enjoying passing through. I leaned forward and wrapped my arms around Phoenix's waist, giving him a little squeeze.

"You okay, doll face?" he asked, scaring the absolute shit out of me. I was so absorbed in my own thoughts and the gorgeous views, I completely forgot we were connected via Bluetooth.

"Sorry, your voice startled me," I cleared my throat, my voice a little hoarse from not being used. "I'm fine, just wanted to give you a hug. It's beautiful out here, isn't it?"

"Yeah, it's beautiful, but I'd much rather be closer to civilization," he grumbled.

I leaned back in my seat. I wasn't going to let him spoil my good time. He could grumble and gripe all he wanted, I was going to cherish every moment I could. I pulled out my phone and started snapping pictures. Hopefully, I could print some and have a nice collage for the wall in my drawing room.

I don't know how long I had been lost in my thoughts again—I blamed the lack of sleep—when a cool gust of wind blew, sending shivers down my spine. Glancing around, I noticed that it seemed to be a bit darker than it was before. Still, the scenery was gorgeous, so I snapped a few more pictures with my phone. Making the decision to be a complete and total dork, I flipped to the front camera and held my phone up to take a selfie. When I looked down at the picture, I gasped.

"Phoenix! It looks like there's a bad storm behind us!" I shouted into my helmet.

"Yeah, I know," he said nonchalantly. I huffed and started to lay into him when he spoke again. "It's not like I have a lot of options right now. I can drive and hope we outrun it, or we can stop and wait for it to pass. Seeing as how I haven't seen a single building in the last 30 miles, I thought you'd appreciate it if I kept driving."

The wind picked up and the sky darkened, but we kept going. I leaned forward and pressed myself against Phoenix's back. We didn't have many storms on the west coast, and I didn't much care for the handful we did have. I wasn't exactly scared, but I had a bad feeling about the storm. I tried to stay positive and remind myself that at least it wasn't raining.

CHAPTER TWENTY-FOUR

Phoenix

I knew the moment she noticed the storm behind us. I felt her whole body tense. Then, she was busting my eardrum screaming at me about it. I noticed a change in the atmosphere a good 20 minutes before she did. I didn't tell her because there was no reason to alert her if it turned out to be nothing. Once I realized it was going to be something, it was just a matter of when she noticed.

At first, I wasn't concerned in the slightest about it. I'd ridden through many storms over the years. It wasn't my favorite thing to do, but the weather was a fickle bitch and sometimes your ass got rained on.

As the miles passed with no sign of civilization, my concern grew exponentially. The wind was getting stronger by the minute. I glanced in my mirror to check the storm's progression, and there was no mistaking what was behind us. The textbook definition of a funnel cloud was rotating in the distance.

"Annabelle, get on your phone and see if you can find somewhere nearby for us to pull off and take shelter," I ordered.

I felt her shifting around behind me. I kept going while I waited for her to find something. Her shaky voice came through the speaker, "I don't see anything, Phoenix. There's nothing around here. What are we going to do?"

Fuck.

Fuck.

Fuck.

I scanned the area for anything we could use for shelter. "Annabelle, I'm going to keep moving as long as I can. Start looking for anything we can use for shelter, and I mean anything. We don't have a lot of time to find something."

We'd made it another mile or so when the wind rocked the bike. She screamed, I grunted, and by the Grace of God we stayed upright.

Fuck. This.

We had to get off the road and off the bike, or we were going to end up dead.

I was slowing down, preparing to tell her we couldn't go any farther when I saw it. Just up ahead, there was a creek that appeared to flow under the road. I sped up, trying my damnedest to get us there.

When we got close enough, I took the bike off the road and drove us right into the culvert. I tapped Annabelle's leg. "Come on, doll face, we need to get off the bike."

I took her hand and pulled her to the middle of the culvert with me. I left my bike just inside the opening we entered, hoping it might shield us from flying debris and prevent the culvert from turning into a wind tunnel. We clung to each other and pressed ourselves as far against the side of the culvert as we could. "I'm scared, Nix," she whimpered. Nix. She was the one and only person to ever call me Nix, and I loved it.

I ran my hand over her hair, trying to comfort her as best I could. "I know, doll face. It'll be over soon." She started crying and tried to pull me even closer. I pressed soft kisses to her forehead and cheeks all the while murmuring words of comfort to her, which did not seem to help her in the slightest. So, I gave my next tactic a try.

Distraction.

"Do you remember when we went to the party Badger threw when his parents were out of town?" I asked.

"Who?"

I chuckled. "Sorry. Aaron Marshall. He's my VP and goes by Badger now."

"Oh! How could I possibly forget that night? It was horrible!"

I laughed. "It wasn't horrible. It was fucking hilarious. It is still the funniest damn thing I have ever experienced firsthand. I love telling that story. You want to hear my version of it?" She nodded against my chest.

The wind was howling through the culvert, rain and hail falling from the sky, accompanied by cracks of thunder and flashes of lightning, as I retold one of my favorite memories with her. "We had been at Badger's parents' place for a few hours, and I'd had too much to drink to drive us home. Instead of staying there for the night, you wanted to drive us home in my truck. We pulled up to a stop sign and just before you pressed the gas pedal, this ball of fur and teeth comes flying at us and slams into the windshield. You started screaming while trying to roll up the windows, close the sliding rear window, and lock the doors at the same time. Then, you started yelling at me because I wasn't helping you, and we were 'under attack.' That was about the time you noticed the ball of fur at the bottom of the windshield. Screaming like a banshee, again, you hit the windshield wipers to fling it off."

I had to pause there to get my laughter under control so I could continue. "You panicked and turned the wipers on, thinking it would knock the thing off the truck. But, you didn't know the thing was stuck. So, when the wipers came on, bat wings shot out of the furball, moving at an arc in front of us. You were screaming, and it was screeching with each pass of the wipers. Eek! Eek! Eek! I thought I was going to piss myself."

She huffed. "I wanted to hit you. I thought it was one of those dinosaur creatures from that movie. You know, the little one everybody thought was cute until it came at them teeth first. Whatever it was, I just wanted to get it away from me as fast as possible. How was I to know it was stuck in the windshield wipers?"

She slapped her hand against my chest. "Then, you wouldn't help me get it out!"

"Of course, I wouldn't. The damn thing was still alive. Plus, bats are usually very precise. The fact that it dive-bombed my truck meant something was wrong. It probably had rabies. But, even though I wouldn't get rid of it, I did provide you with a way to get it out of the wipers, didn't I?"

She slapped her hand against my chest. "Giving me $20 to pay the crackhead at the gas station to pluck it out of the wipers with your jumper cables doesn't count, Phoenix Black!"

Tears were running down my face from laughing. That story never got old. "It most certainly does count. He took care of the bat, we went home, and all was well...except you refused to drive at night after that for a long time. Wait a minute. Are you laughing?"

She pushed her face under my arm to hide it from me, but I could feel her body shaking. I pushed her back so I could see her. She was always beautiful, but when she laughed, she was like nothing I had ever seen before.

"Okay. You win. It is a funny story."

I suddenly had the overwhelming urge to kiss her, and I didn't see any reason why I shouldn't. I cupped the back of her neck and pulled her lips to mine. The kiss started off slow and gentle, but soon became hungry and full of need.

A loud crash broke us apart. Wide-eyed and panting, Annabelle cautiously asked, "What was that?"

My jaw clenched as I looked over her shoulder and stared at the space where my bike used to be. "I'm guessing it was my bike."

She whirled around to see for herself. "Fucking fuck! What are we going to do?"

"Calm down, doll face. When it's safe, we'll go find my bike and see if it's still drivable. If it is, we'll ride to the closest town and get a room for the night. I'll look over the bike, and hopefully, we can be on our way in the morning. If it's not drivable, we'll call for a tow truck. We'll still get a room for the night, and I'll see about renting a cage and trailer to haul it back home," I explained.

We stayed put for 10 more minutes or so before we ventured out of the culvert to survey the damage. We found the tangled mess of metal that used to be my bike about 100 yards from the culvert.

"I don't think that's drivable," Annabelle observed. If that was my actual bike, my baby, I would have been losing my shit right then, but luckily it wasn't. I kept a few bikes at the clubhouse as loaners when needed. I opted to take one that would provide a more comfortable ride across the country, especially if I found her and convinced her to come back with me.

I sighed. "Let's see about getting a tow truck to come get us."

After discovering that neither one of our cell phones had service, we grabbed what we could from the bike and started walking. I didn't have a clue how far we would have to walk before we found people or cell phone reception.

It was hot as hell, we had no food and very little water. I was good to go for a while, but I was worried Annabelle wouldn't be able to keep up and push forward. As if on cue, Annabelle said, "Phoenix, I need to stop for just a minute."

I whirled around, ready to tell her she couldn't start whining this early in our trek, to find her bent down, digging through her backpack. "Aha!" she exclaimed, pulling something out of her bag. She promptly removed her jeans and slid on a tiny pair of cutoff shorts. Then, she stripped her top half down to a tank top, crammed everything into her bag, and smiled brightly. "Much better. Continue on." She looked sexy as fuck wearing her riding boots with that outfit. Yeah, she would be wearing that for me again when I had time to show her my appreciation.

We continued on for several miles, checking our phones every now and then for service. Finally, after almost three hours of walking, we saw a house in the distance. Hopefully, the occupants would have some means of communication.

When we were closer to the house, we saw that only the front half of the house was intact. The back was completely obliterated, as was a barn and another structure that was no longer identifiable. I told Annabelle to stay back while I walked closer. The house could collapse at any second, and I didn't want her anywhere near it.

"Hello!" I called out. "Anyone there?"

Silence.

"Hello!" I called again.

"Phoenix, look!" Annabelle yelled, pointing at something. "I think that's a door to a storm shelter."

I walked over to where she was pointing, and sure enough, there was a door in the ground. I assumed it led to a storm shelter, but after discovering the numerous hidden rooms and tunnels on the farm property, it could be a door to anything.

Annabelle reached for the handle. and I immediately grabbed her wrist. "Don't!" I barked sternly. "If anyone is in there, they're likely not expecting company. You might open that door to find yourself face-to-face with the business end of a shotgun."

She huffed but stepped back. I gave the door three sharp knocks and called out, "Hello? Anyone there?"

Moments later, a very young sounding voice answered, "Who's there?"

"My name is Phoenix, and I'm here with Annabelle. We've been stranded due to the storm, and we're looking for somewhere we could call for help. This is the first place we've come upon."

Several beats passed before the child spoke again. "Um...we're not supposed to open the door unless it's Mommy or Daddy or Judy."

Annabelle brought her hand to her mouth and took a step forward. "Are you in there by yourself, sweetheart?"

"No, ma'am. My brother is in here, too. Judy put us in here and went back to the house. You can knock on the door and ask to use the phone. And ask her if we can come out now. Please."

"Who is Judy?" Annabelle asked.

"Our babysitter. Daddy's at work, and Mommy had appointments today."

I pinched the bridge of my nose and sighed. Things didn't sound promising where Judy was concerned. She was probably somewhere in the house, which was on the verge of collapsing.

"Phoenix," Annabelle whispered, "we have to go look for her. She might be hurt."

"She might be, but she could just as well be dead. That house isn't stable, and neither one of us are going in there." She opened her mouth to argue, but I held up my hand to stop her. Turning my attention to the door, I asked, "Do you have a phone or something in there to call for emergencies?"

"Yes, sir. There's a radio talkie thing my daddy used during a storm one time. I don't know how to work it though."

"Does your brother know how to use it?"

The little girl giggled. "No, he's just a baby."

My eyes widened. I turned my head to see that Annabelle's eyes mirrored mine. "They can't stay in there by themselves," Annabelle whispered. I knew that, but the little girl was right to not open the door to strangers.

Annabelle cleared her throat and spoke softly to the door, "Sweetheart, I know your parents told you not to open the door to strangers, and they are right about that, but this is a very special situation. Did your Mommy and Daddy ever tell you what to do if there was an emergency and they weren't with you?"

The little girl answered immediately, "Yes,

ma'am. Mommy told me if I ever got lost or needed help and she wasn't there to find a lady that looked like a mommy and ask her to help me."

Annabelle smiled. "Your mommy is very smart. That's exactly what I told my son to do. So, since I'm a mommy and you need help, will you open the door so I can help you?"

The girl was silent, apparently thinking over Annabelle's offer. Surprising us both, the little girl came back with, "How do I know you're a mommy?"

Annabelle laughed again. "Well, I suppose you don't, but let me see if I can prove it." She took in a deep breath and squared her shoulders. "First, I have three children. Their names are Ember, Coal, and Nathan. Ember and Coal are twins. Now, I'm going to tell you some things that only mommies do. When our child is in trouble, we call them by their whole name. We count to three, sometimes five, when our child is about to get into trouble. We won't let you ruin your dinner with cookies and sweets. We make you clean your room when you don't want to. We make you feel better when you're sick, and we love you more than anything in the world. Does that sound about right?"

The door to the storm shelter slowly started to open as the little girl struggled to push it open. I quickly grabbed the handle and opened it the rest of the way. The little girl popped her head out and said, "If you know all that, you must really be a mommy." She was a beautiful child, maybe five or six years old, with wild blonde hair and big brown eyes.

Annabelle smiled. "I am, sweetheart. Now, can you show me where that radio talkie thing is? I bet Phoenix here knows how to work it."

The girl's eyes darted to me, full of trepidation. I was a big man, and there was no way to hide it. Grown men found my size intimidating; I was likely nothing short of a monster to a frightened young child. I squatted down hoping to seem less intimidating to her. "Why don't you go get your little brother and bring him out here with Annabelle? Then, I'll go down and see about the radio. That way you haven't broken any of your parents' rules."

She thought that over for a minute and then nodded her head resolutely. "I'll be right back." She returned with her arms wrapped tightly around the middle of a squirming baby boy. It looked like she was squeezing the hell out of him, and he wasn't the least bit happy about it.

Annabelle reached out to help her with the baby. "Does he have a diaper bag down there or anything like that?"

"Yes, ma'am. I'll go get it," she said as she eyed me.

"I'll stay right here," I promised.

She returned, struggling to carry the big bag up the stairs. I reached my hand out slowly. "I can take the bag for you, dear."

She exhaled in relief. "Thank you, mister."

Once Annabelle had the kids settled on a blanket, I entered the storm shelter in search of what I guessed was a CB radio. I found it sitting on a shelf along the back wall. It had been a long time since I had used a CB, but I figured it couldn't be too difficult to use. I turned the radio on and began scanning through the channels. It didn't take long to find one filled with voices reporting damage from the tornado. I listened for a few minutes before speaking. I told them about mine and Annabelle's situation as well as the situation we discovered at the farmhouse. The response I received was not at all what I had hoped for.

I left the storm shelter to find Annabelle trying to soothe the little girl who was sobbing. "What happened?" I asked quietly.

Annabelle grimaced. "She saw the house."
I glanced up and had a very clear view of the destroyed half of the house. I didn't know what to do. I was a stranger to the little girl, and she had seemed somewhat scared of me earlier. I wanted to comfort her, but wasn't sure that I should. Annabelle interrupted my internal battle with her question, "Did you have any luck with the radio?"

"If you mean, did I get it to work? Yes, I did. Is help on the way? Eventually."

"Eventually? What exactly does that mean?"

I sighed. "It means that the storm did a lot of damage in the surrounding area. Emergency crews are working their way through it all, but it could take them up to 72 hours to get to us. Since there is no one here with injuries, we aren't a priority."

"What about the children?" she asked.

"I explained that, and I was told that we should stay with the kids until their parents or help arrived."

She looked at me with disbelief in her eyes. "You've got to be kidding."

"Sorry, doll face," I shrugged. "Looks like we're staying here for a bit."

CHAPTER TWENTY-FIVE

Annabelle

I tried to make the best out of a bad situation. What else could I do? There was no way Phoenix or I would have ever left those children to fend for themselves. I just hoped their parents saw it that way, too. I wasn't sure how I would have reacted to finding strangers hunkered down with Nathan when he was younger.

Over the course of the afternoon, I learned that the little girl was named Charlie, and she was five and a half years old. Her little brother was Austin, and he was six months old.

Charlie cried for quite a while when she saw the state of their house, but she finally calmed down when I assured her that we wouldn't leave her and Austin alone. It took some time, but she eventually warmed up to Phoenix, too.

We spent the afternoon and well into the evening playing outside. Phoenix even brought some food out of the storm shelter and made a picnic for us. I tended to the baby, who was surprisingly calm and content, especially given the fact that he was being cared for by strangers.

When the sun started to set, we went into the storm shelter to get settled down for the night. It was much larger than I expected, about the size of a shipping container. It had all the necessary items to keep us comfortable for far longer than three days. There was even a small bathroom!

"Annabelle," Charlie asked as she tugged on my shirt, "will you tuck me in after I brush my teeth?"

I smiled down at her. "Of course, I will. Do you need help brushing your teeth?"

She shook her head. "No, ma'am, I'm a big girl."

Once Charlie was tucked in and Austin was down for the night, I hoped, I took a seat on the small sofa beside Phoenix. "You're awfully quiet."

"Just wondering how this is going to play out. Don't you think their parents should have been here by now?" he asked.

Yes, I did think that, if they were able. "They might be hurt, or maybe the roads are blocked, or maybe they got stranded like we did," I suggested.

He gave me a pointed look. "Both of them? Likely not. Besides, wouldn't you fight tooth and nail to get back to your kids?"

I slowly nodded my head. "Yes, I would, but we don't know what happened, and we don't have any way of knowing. Don't forget, they probably assume the kids are with their babysitter. There's no use in getting worked up over speculation."

I stood and extended my hand. "Come on, let's try to get some sleep."

***

Something startled me from my sleep. When I sat up and rubbed the sleep from my eyes, Phoenix was already on his feet heading toward the door. I heard the door rattle and a frantic male voice shout, "Charlie! It's Daddy!! Open the door, honey!"

I sighed with relief. At least one parent was alive and well. It had taken me a long time to fall asleep because I couldn't stop worrying about the children's parents.

Phoenix slowly opened the door. The man on the other side morphed from frantic to furious in a nanosecond. "Who the fuck are you and where are my children?"

Phoenix held his hands up and took a few steps back. "Just calm down, man. Your kids are right through there, and they're fine."

The man stormed down the stairs and marched right past Phoenix and I. He was visibly relieved at the sight of his sleeping children, but he was no less furious. He whirled around. "Again, who the fuck are you?"

Phoenix remained calm, or he appeared to remain calm on the outside. I knew him though, and judging by his stance and the tick in his jaw, he was ready for an attack. "My name is Phoenix Black, and this is Annabelle Burnett," he gestured to me. "We were stranded after the storm, and your place was the first home we came upon. We were just looking for a way to call for help when we found the children in the storm shelter."

The man fumed. "So you just invited yourself in here, WITH MY KIDS?"

Charlie's soft voice filled the room, "Daddy? Why are you yelling at my friends?"

"They're not your friends, Charlie."

Charlie walked closer to her father. "Yes, they are, Daddy. They helped me and Austin. If they weren't here, we would've been all alone. I didn't let them in right away. I talked to them through the door first. Ms. Annabelle is a mommy, and Mommy always told me to go to another mommy if I needed help. So, that's what I did." She crossed her arms and leveled him with a look that dared him to say her actions were wrong. Before he could speak, she continued, "Mr. Phoenix even stayed outside and waited for me to bring Austin out. Then, he went to get the talkie radio. I was scared of him at first, but that was silly. He's a really nice man, Daddy. He's tried to call for help a lot of times, but they just keep telling him they'll get here when they can since no one is hurt."

The man blinked several times before scooping his daughter into his arms. He turned to face us. "That true?"

Phoenix nodded. "Yes. I tried several times to get someone to either come out here or try to get in touch with either one of their parents. I didn't have any luck with that. The responders told us to stay with the children until help arrived. We wouldn't have left them alone in the first place, but you might want to speak to the appropriate officials about advising random strangers to watch after someone else's kids."

The man sighed. "Thank you for looking after them. I apologize for my initial reaction."

"No apologies necessary. You had every right to react that way to finding strangers hunkered down with your children. You've got a very smart little girl right there," Phoenix said and grinned at Charlie.

The man smiled. "Don't I know it. Oh, forgive me, it's been quite a day." He extended his hand to Phoenix. "I'm Curtis Smith."

After shaking hands with Phoenix, Curtis turned to me and did the same. "I would say it's a pleasure to meet you, but under the circumstances..."

"I completely understand," I said. "If I may, is your wife okay? Charlie said she was out running errands when the tornado hit."

He put Charlie down and instructed her to go back to bed. "She's in the hospital. The building she was in collapsed, and she was trapped in the rubble. She'll be okay though. Other than a mild concussion, it's mainly just bumps and bruises, but she's three months pregnant, so they wanted to keep her overnight to monitor the baby."

I fidgeted with my hands before asking, "Charlie mentioned the babysitter, Judy, went back to the house after getting them to the shelter. Any word on her?"

Curtis grimaced. "She was found about a quarter mile from here. She's alive, but unconscious and in critical condition. As soon as I heard she was brought in with no sign of the children, I got here as fast as I could."

"I'm sorry to hear that," I said softly.

After a brief pause, Curtis clapped his hands. "Well, is there something I can do to help you two? You said you were stranded after the storm?"

Phoenix filled him in on our tornado experience. "I just need to find somewhere to rent something I can haul my bike back home with."

"You're not going to have any luck around here, but I can drive you a few towns over to get something."

"Thanks, man. I'd greatly appreciate that," Phoenix replied.

"We can head out now if Annabelle doesn't mind staying with the kids."

"I'd be happy to," I told them. I wasn't sure of the time, but I figured the kids would sleep for a while longer.

Four hours later, Phoenix and Curtis returned, Phoenix driving a rented box truck. Curtis helped him get the bike loaded into the truck and we said our goodbyes. Charlie was quite upset about our departure, but I promised to call in a day or two to check in with her and her family. We offered to stay and help Curtis, but he said there would be nothing to do for several days. With a final hug goodbye, Phoenix and I climbed into the truck and continued on our journey back to Croftridge.

CHAPTER TWENTY-SIX

Phoenix

"You okay?" I asked. Annabelle had been quiet since we left Curtis, Charlie, and Austin.

"Yes, I'm fine," she replied, quickly. A little too quickly I thought.

"Don't lie to me, doll face. I'll pull this truck over if I have to," I warned.

She rolled her eyes. "I was just thinking about our children," she paused, "and how much I missed of their lives," she finished on a sob.

I eased the truck off the highway and pulled her into my arms. Rubbing her back, I soothed, "I know it's hard, but you can't dwell on that part of it. I know how you feel, doll face, I truly do, but you have to let that part go. We can't change the past, no matter how much we wish we could."

She balled up her fists and beat them against my chest. "I hate him! I hate him! I wish he wasn't dead so I could kill him myself! He took so much from me! From us!"

I held her close and rocked her back and forth. "He can't take anything else away from us. That I can promise you."

She leaned away from me and wiped her eyes. "I'm sorry. This past week has wreaked havoc on my emotions."

"It's okay, doll face. Don't ever hide your feelings from me." I leaned forward and kissed her lips. I intended to give her a chaste kiss, a quick hug, and get back on the road. Instead, Annabelle pulled me closer, thrust her tongue into my mouth, and climbed into my lap. The next thing I knew, she had her lower half stripped bare and my jeans open.

"I need you, Phoenix," she breathed. Then, she held my cock in one hand, raised herself up, and slid down, all the while staring into my eyes. She rode the hell out of me in that box truck on the side of the road, using my body to work out her frustrations. Moaning and groaning, her hips rising and falling, she didn't stop until we were both coming at the same time.

Leaning forward, I pressed my forehead against hers. "Feel better?"

She licked her lips and whispered, "Yes."

I grinned. "Good. You start feeling down again, you just let me know, yeah?" I winked.

***

I decided to stop in St. Louis for the night. I probably could have made it back to Croftridge without stopping, but having Annabelle all to myself for one more night sounded too good to pass up.

Once again, I chose one of the nicer hotels, though this time I hadn't been able to plan for any surprises ahead of time. Once we were settled in our room, Annabelle suggested we order room service instead of going out for dinner. That sounded like a great plan to me. As much as I didn't want to admit it, I was fucking exhausted.

After dinner, Annabelle informed me that she was going to take a bath. I figured I could use the time to call and check in with Ember and Coal, as well as touch base with Badger. I was just about to hit Ember's name when I heard,

"Phoenix? Can you come here for a second?"

I strolled into the bathroom to find a large garden tub in the corner the bathroom with a smiling Annabelle submerged up to her neck in bubbles. When her eyes landed on mine, she stood and let the bubbles slide down her glorious body.

"Care to join me, biker boy?" she asked while crooking her finger at me.

I grinned. "Fuck yes," I growled. I quickly shed my clothes and prowled toward my sudsy goddess. When I reached the tub, I stepped in, yanked her soapy body against mine, and devoured her mouth.

Groaning against her lips, I slid my hands down to cup her luscious tits. I lightly rubbed my thumbs over her nipples while she moaned and squirmed in my arms.

She broke the kiss, and before I could register what she was doing, she was on her knees, sucking the head of my cock into her hot little mouth. "Annabelle," I hissed, clenching both fists in her hair.

She wrapped her fist around the base of my cock and continued sliding her mouth up and down my shaft at a slow pace. "Fuck, Annabelle, you're going to have to stop. Your mouth feels too fucking good."

She didn't stop. She kept going and increased her pace. When I heard and felt her moan, my eyes flew open, and I looked down to see my fantasy from a few days before coming true right before my very eyes. Annabelle was on her knees in the tub, going to town on my cock while one of her hands was steadily moving between her legs. And the motherfucking bubbles were blocking my view.

"Don't you dare fucking come," I growled. She blinked up at me and grinned, never once breaking her rhythm.

"Fuck, baby, I'm going to come," I groaned and tried to pull her head away from me. She'd swallowed my seed many times when we were teenagers, but I didn't know how she felt about it as an adult. She clamped her lips around me, sucked harder, and that was it. I exploded, shooting strand after strand down her throat.

She licked me clean and looked up at me, grinning like the Cheshire cat. With a speed she wasn't prepared for, I hoisted her up, planted her ass on the corner edge of the tub, and dropped to my knees. "My turn," I growled and shoved my face between her legs.

With her pinned in the corner, she had to put

her legs over my shoulders and use one hand to brace herself against the wall. The other hand had a fistful of my hair. I licked, flicked, nibbled, and sucked her as she writhed against me. When she started to beg, I shoved two fingers into her and crooked them forward as I roughly pumped them in and out of her until she was coming all over my face with my name on her lips.

By the time she found her release, I was hard as fucking steel again. I sat back in the tub and pulled her into my lap, lifting her enough to position myself at her entrance. We both groaned when she slid down my cock, inch by agonizing inch.

"Phoenix," she breathed.

I grabbed her ass with both hands and grunted, "Fucking bounce, baby."

And bounce she did. Water was sloshing everywhere, and I was probably leaving finger shaped bruises on her ass cheeks, but I didn't give a fuck. My dick was getting the ride of its life while my face was buried between the best set of tits I'd ever seen.

"Oh, shit. Fuck, Phoenix. I'm going to come again."

"Let me have it, baby. Fucking come all over me."

She slammed her hips down on me two more times before I felt the walls of her pussy rippling with her orgasm. Clasping her hips, I moved her up and down half a dozen more times before I followed her over the edge.

She kissed me softly and moved to nuzzle against my neck. "You okay, doll face?"

"Mmm-hmm," she replied, sounding sleepy and content.

"Come on, baby, let's get cleaned up and get some sleep. We'll be home tomorrow."

CHAPTER TWENTY-SEVEN

Annabelle

My nerves were frazzled. The closer we got to Croftridge, the faster my heart beat. I could feel cold beads of sweat forming on my forehead and down my spine. By the time we rolled into Croftridge, I was a sweaty, hyperventilating mess a few heartbeats short of a full-blown panic attack.

"Calm down, Annabelle. Everything's going to be just fine, I promise," Phoenix said, startling me and causing me to jump about six inches off my seat.

Easy for him to say. He'd already done the meet and greet with our long lost children, and he got to do it without a week's worth of anticipation.

Chewing off the last sliver of the only fingernail I had left, I asked, "Where are we going?"

"I'm taking you to my house first. It's Pop's and Gram's house. I thought you might want to freshen up, and then we'll figure things out from there. I can have the kids come over to my house, we can go to Ember's house, or we can all meet up at the clubhouse, whichever you prefer."

I didn't want to meet them at the clubhouse because I knew we would have a large audience there, and I most certainly did not want that. I thought I recalled Phoenix saying Ember lived on the farm property, and I had no interest in going back to that hellhole, not yet anyway. That only left us with one option. "I guess it would be best if they came to your house."

He reached over and gave my leg a gentle squeeze. "Okay, doll face, if that's what you want, that's what we'll do."

He pulled into the driveway of the old plantation style home I remembered so well. It looked just the same as it did the last time I saw it. The house was huge and screamed of money, but it was also warm and inviting.

Phoenix came around and opened my door for me, extending his hand to help me climb out of the truck. He cupped my cheeks and kissed the tip of my nose, then held my hand as he led me to the front door.

Before he turned the knob, the front door flew open, and there stood two people with faces I hadn't seen in 13 years but instantly recognized, Ember and Coal. No one moved. No one said a word, for a very long time. We all just stared at one another.

Finally, Phoenix broke the silence. He cleared his throat and said, "Ember, Coal, this is your mother, Annabelle."

My eyes flicked from Phoenix to my grown children. I didn't have time to process anything else before both of them slammed into my body, wrapping their arms around my shoulders and my waist. "Mom," they both cried at the same time.

That was when the dam burst. I sunk to the floor with both of them, sobbing and gasping for air. "I'm so sorry," I said between my broken cries. "I'm so sorry! I didn't know. I never would have—"

"It's okay, Mom," Ember said.

Coal nodded. "We know what happened. It's not anyone's fault but Octavius's."

I searched both of their faces. "You really believe that?"

"Yes," and "Of course, we do," they replied at the same time.

"How about we go inside, yeah?" Phoenix suggested.

The kids got to their feet, and Phoenix helped me to mine. We all moved into the house to continue our reunion. I took a seat on the couch, Phoenix settling down right beside me. He put his arm around my shoulder and gave it a squeeze. "So, kids, want to tell me why you were in my house when I got back?"

Coal and Ember both laughed, but it was Ember that answered, "Because we're not stupid, Dad. I haven't been around all that long, but in the time I have been around the club, no one has ever gone on a solo run, especially for the length of time you said you would be gone. Plus, your son is a part of the club, and those bikers gossip worse than most women."

"I see. Does Dash know you're here?"

"Nope," she said, popping the p, "but I'll text him now and let him know where I am."

I sat there quietly observing their interactions. The three of them seemed very comfortable with one another, which should have comforted me, but it had the opposite effect. I felt like an outsider, a stranger. Suddenly, I felt like I was suffocating in that room, and I desperately needed a moment to compose myself. Quietly, I excused myself to the restroom.

Once I was behind the safety of the closed door, I finally let out the breath that had been trapped in my chest. I knew I didn't have much time to get myself together before I needed to go back out there and face them, talk to them, but I just couldn't get a handle on myself. As if on cue, there was a knock on the door.

I braced myself and pulled the door open, fully expecting Phoenix to push his way into the bathroom with me. Instead, I was met with Ember's soft face. She gave me a small smile and said, "I have less than two minutes before Dad comes barging in, so I'll get right to it. Coal and I are both glad that you're here. We want to get to know you and have you be a part of our lives. This has to be unbelievably overwhelming, so Coal and I are going to head out soon. I thought maybe tomorrow you and I could spend some time together in the morning, and then you and Coal could spend some time together tomorrow afternoon. That way it doesn't feel like you're under the microscope while you're trying to find your footing."

I pulled her into a hug. "You're a very smart

young woman."

She leaned back and met my eyes. "I know what it feels like. I had the whole club watching when Dad and I were trying to develop a relationship, and then again with Coal. It was stressful, to say the least."

I hugged her again and kissed the top of her head. "Thank you for that. I do want to know you and Coal and be a part of your lives, very much. I think I'm just scared to believe this is really happening. It was hard when I lost Phoenix, but it almost killed me when I lost you. If I had known about Coal back then, it probably would have killed me. I can't go through a loss like that again."

"It's real, I promise." She squeezed me tighter and sighed. "I'm so glad he found you."

"Me, too, baby girl. Me, too."

When Ember and I returned from the bathroom, we ran into Phoenix in the hallway. She was right. He was on his way to barge in and solve problems. The four of us sat and talked casually for another 30 minutes or so before the kids left. I made plans to spend the following morning with Ember and the afternoon with Coal. Unfortunately, to do so meant I had to go back to the farm, and that was something I wholeheartedly did not want to do.

I was fairly quiet for the rest of the evening. Blessedly, Phoenix didn't push for me to talk. Of all the things to process from the last week of my life, the one thing that kept cycling through my mind was going back to the farm. Years ago, I promised myself if I ever got away from that dreadful place I would never return. At the time, I had no idea I would one day have grown children happily living on the property.

"You okay, doll face?" Phoenix's deep rumble caused me to jolt.

"Yeah, just tired. I think I'm going to take a shower and go to bed," I answered, hoping he believed my lie. He didn't.

"Know you're lying to me, doll face. What I don't know is why..." he trailed off expecting me to answer.

I huffed. "My world has been completely upended this past week. I met my children, as my children, for the first time today. Not to mention we just rode halfway across the country on a motorcycle, survived a tornado, and drove the rest of the way in a box truck. I think I have a right to be tired!"

He stalked closer to me. "Yeah, you do have a right to be tired, but none of the things you just spewed has anything to do with what's bothering you. You gonna tell me or do I need to make you?"

"Fuck off, Phoenix. Don't you dare talk to me like I'm a child!" I yelled.

He placed his hands on my hips and held me in place. "Then stop acting like one and start talking."

I turned my head to the side and muttered, "I don't want to go to the farm."

He engulfed me with his arms. "Oh, baby, I didn't realize you were scared to go back there."

"I'm not scared. I just don't want to."

He lightly chuckled. "You're scared, and that's okay. Listen, Ember and Coal live there. Do you think I would let my kids live somewhere that wasn't safe?" He didn't wait for me to answer. "A few of the club members work for Ember and some even live out there. Kathleen and Jeff still live there. Plus, a lot of things have changed. Parts of it don't even look the same."

I knew he was trying to help, but there was little to nothing he could say that would make me feel any better about the whole thing. Or so I thought.

"How about I go with you? Not to hover over you and the kids, but just so you know I'm there.

We'll ride over in my truck, and you can keep the keys so you can leave whenever you want," he offered.

I nodded into his chest. "That sounds good."

He took a step back and met my eyes. "All right, now that that's settled, you need to check your phone before you get in the shower. It's been ringing a lot. It's downstairs in your bag. Want me to get it for you?"

When he returned with my bag, I picked up my phone to look at the missed calls, but it started ringing in my hand.

"Hello," I answered, inwardly cringing when I realized who had been calling.

"Hell, girl, you've damn near given me a heart attack! I haven't heard from you in days. Token and I were getting ready to come looking for you!" Wave barked into the phone.

"I'm so sorry! I'm fine, really. The trip didn't go as expected, but we made it to Croftridge a few hours ago," I rushed out.

"I see. Well, start talking, half pint. Tell me all about it."

I was on the phone with Wave for well over an hour. He was like the father I never had but always wished for. He wasn't old enough to be my father, but that was the role he played in my life.

By the time we were finished, I was exhausted. I sent a quick text to Nathan and decided to skip the shower. Minutes later I was fast asleep.

CHAPTER TWENTY-EIGHT

Annabelle

Phoenix held my hand with a firm grip as we approached the gates to the farm. He was right, the place did look different, but that didn't stop my mind from telling me to run as far and as fast as I could from the Gates of Hell.

"What's with the guards at the gate?" I asked.

He grimaced and shifted in his seat. "We had a situation a month or so ago, and the club decided having men on the gate was the best way to secure the property."

I stiffened. "What kind of situation?"

He sighed, clearly not wanting to tell me. "My club brother's kid was kidnapped by his estranged wife's sister. Kathleen was watching him when he was taken. We never figured out how she got onto the property, so I put measures in place to make sure no one else unwanted could get in here."

We drove past the place where Octavius's house used to be, the place I used to live, and I was shocked to see nothing but grass. The words were out of my mouth before I could stop them. "Where's the house?"

Phoenix laughed, but it was a laugh filled with hate. "Blew that fucker up the first chance I got."

I smiled. "Good." Learning that the house I was forced to live in with Octavius was gone relieved some of my fear about returning to the farm.

We pulled up to a house on the property that had not been there during the years I spent on the farm. "This is where Ember and Dash live. You go on up, and I'll go busy myself in my office. If you need me, just call my cell or Ember can show you where the office is. See you this evening, doll face." He gave me a kiss on the cheek and strolled away while I fought the urge to wrap my limbs around his leg like a child and beg him to stay with me.

It took me several minutes to get myself

together enough to get out of the truck. I warily approached the house, waiting for some unforeseen boogie man to jump out and grab me. Raising my shaking hand, I lightly knocked on the door.

I was in the middle of arguing with myself about staying versus running back to the car and high-tailing it out of there when the door opened. A very handsome young man smiled at me and opened the door wider. "You must be Annabelle. I'm Ember's fiancé, Dash. Please come in. Ember is finishing up in the kitchen. She'll be right out."

I followed the young man into their living room and glanced around. They had a beautiful home. I couldn't help but notice that the decor was eerily similar to my house in California. Like mother, like daughter, I thought.

Ember came through a door on the other side of the room, wiping her hands on a frilly and flirty apron. Before I could comment on it, she smiled and said, "Morning, Mom. Would you like some breakfast?"

My heart fluttered. She called me Mom. She did it the day before, but this time seemed different somehow. I cleared the emotion from my throat and answered, "Yes, breakfast would be lovely."

Dash joined us for breakfast, but left soon after. I was prepared for a morning filled with tension and awkward silences; however, there was none of that. Ember gave me a tour of her horse farm and then her organic plants project. It was truly impressive what she had done with a space that was once used for nothing but creating misery.

After we circled the rear portion of the property and were back at her house, she said, "I know Dad already told you how we found each other and everything that happened afterward, but what happened to you? I remember you from when I was little. You were there one morning and gone that afternoon. I tried to ask about you, but I was told to never say your name."

Her words brought tears to my eyes. She remembered me, and she asked about me. That meant she missed me. I inhaled deeply before I answered. "The day I disappeared was the day I finally escaped from Octavius. If I had known you were mine, I would have taken you with me, but at the time, I believed you were at the daycare while your parents worked on the farm. They even told me your name was Amber, not Ember."

"I know you didn't intentionally leave me behind. Please believe me when I tell you that I do not harbor one negative thought or feeling about you. None of this was anyone's fault except Octavius's. He destroyed our family; no one else is to blame," she said vehemently.

But she didn't know that I did take one of my kids with me. I needed to tell her and get it over with. The longer I kept it from her, the harder it would be for her to accept it. "I have to tell you something."

"Nivan's my brother, isn't he?" she asked.

My eyes widened in shock. How did she know about him? What did she know about him? "Yes, he is. He goes by Nathan now, though."

"What?" she shrieked. "He's alive?"

I was taken aback by her reaction. "Yes, he's alive. He's been with me in California the whole time. Why did you think he was dead?"

She shook her head in disbelief. "Because that's what Octavius's right-hand man, Hector, told us. Octavius did a very good job of hiding the truth about him. I thought that he was alive and living on the farm, but then Hector said that Nivan died when he was five years old and there was documentation to prove it, though it was never found. No one ever said different, so I assumed he really was dead."

"I see. Well, when I disappeared years ago, I took Nathan with me. A friend helped me fake an accident, and then some people at the hospital helped us get away. He had just turned five years old at the time."

Suddenly, I felt compelled to defend Nathan. "He's nothing like Octavius. He doesn't even know about him. He thinks his father was a Marine who died while deployed. He's a good person. He's the only reason I didn't give up years ago."

She smiled. "I would like to meet him."

"I would like that, too, but I need to tell him about you first. Actually, I need to tell him everything. He doesn't even know I'm here in Croftridge," I explained.

"I understand. I have no intention of disrupting his life or anything like that. I just wanted you to know I want to meet him, whenever you think the time is right."

We spent the rest of the morning talking and getting to know one another. The time went by faster than I expected. I honestly didn't want to leave, but I also wanted to spend a similar afternoon with my son.

"How long are you going to be in Croftridge?"

she asked.

"I'm not sure. My boss said I could take as much time as I needed off work, but I don't want to abuse that offer. Nathan will be home from his training camp in a few weeks, so I will definitely have to be home by then," I answered. Since I wasn't sure how things would play out, I hadn't given much thought to how long I would stay.

Her face fell. "Will you come back here?"

"To visit or to live?"

"Either."

"I will definitely come back to visit, as often as I can. As far as living here...I've built a life for myself in California. I can't just up and leave. But, you're welcome to come visit me whenever you want and stay as long as you like," I said, trying to lift her spirits.

She spoke quietly when she said, "Dash and I have been waiting for Dad to find you or find out what happened to you to get married because I wanted you to be there if you were alive. Do you think you can be here for the wedding?"

"There's no way I would miss it. When do you think it will be?" I asked.

"We would like for it to be sooner rather than later. I think I can pull everything together in two or three weeks. Could you stay in Croftridge that long?" she asked.

"Let me check with my boss and see if I can take that much time off. If he doesn't have a problem with it, then I'll stay until the wedding."

She embraced me with a tight hug. "Thank you! I can't wait to tell Dash!"

Ding-dong.

"Oh, that must be Coal. I'll be right back."

She returned with her twin. "Since Coal either stays at the Martins' house or the clubhouse, I thought it would be easier for you two to talk and get to know one another without an audience so I offered the use of my house. Dash will be gone for the rest of the day, and I have to get to the barn to finish ordering supplies and making out next week's schedule."

With that, she skipped out the door leaving me and Coal alone. He took a seat in the chair but remained silent.

After several moments of uncomfortable silence, I asked, "Do you, um, do you remember me?"

"Yeah," he answered.

"I didn't know about you," I blurted. "I know that sounds crazy, but I was never allowed to see my ultrasounds, and the doctor never talked to me about my pregnancy. It never even occurred to me that I might be pregnant with twins."

He nodded. "I know that."

I waited for him to say more, but he didn't. The ease I had with Ember seemed to have walked out the door with her. "We don't have to do this today. You don't seem very interested in being here." He was not the compassionate and understanding young man from the day before.

He blinked and sat up straighter. "I'm sorry. My wounds are bothering me, and I'm waiting on the medicine to kick in. I guess I overdid it yesterday. It helps to be still and not talk until the pain eases off."

"Oh! You shouldn't have come if you're in pain. We could have done this another day or even later today. What can I do to help you?" I asked. I had unknowingly left my seat and was hovering beside him, well, like a mom.

He grimaced. "Will you hand me one of those pillows?"

I quickly grabbed a throw pillow and handed it to him. He braced it across his abdomen and said, "Let's watch something on television for a bit. I should be fine in about 30 minutes."

We watched some show about cars for the next hour. When it ended, he turned the television off with the remote and said, "Sorry about that. I'm feeling much better now. What would you like to do for the rest of the afternoon?"

I had no idea what my options were. I just wanted to spend time with him, but I didn't want him doing anything that would cause him pain, so I told him just that. We opted to stay at Ember's house and talk, which allowed me the opportunity to fuss over him and take care of him.

We spent the afternoon talking, much like Ember and I had. I told him about escaping from Octavius, and then I told him about Nathan. He was also interested in meeting his half-brother, particularly once I told him about Nathan's budding MMA career.

He told me about his life growing up on the farm with Kathleen and Jeff. Kathleen was a kind and genuine woman. If I had to choose someone other than myself or Phoenix to raise our children, it would be her. If only Ember could have been adopted by them, too.

Coal told me the story of the shooting from his point of view, and his version was much more harrowing than the version Phoenix told me. I cried all over his shoulder while he hugged me and repeatedly assured me he was okay.

Then, he said something that had been

flitting around in the back of my mind since Phoenix showed up in California. "Mom, I believe everything happens for a reason. I mean, getting shot sucked, but if it hadn't happened, I wouldn't know about my biological family, at least not at this point anyway. Ember and I have talked about this a lot over the last few weeks, and she feels the same way about the events of her life."

"Yeah, I feel the same way about certain aspects of my life as well," I said, unwilling to specifically reference Nathan.

Coal nodded as if he understood what I wasn't saying and blessedly changed the subject.

Before I knew it, Ember had returned to the house with Dash and Phoenix. Apparently, it was well after dinner time, and they refused to stay away any longer. Ember invited Phoenix and me to stay for dinner, but Phoenix politely declined for the both of us. And I was glad he did. The day had gone much better than expected, and I didn't want to push my luck. Phoenix offered to drive Coal back to the clubhouse, but he opted to stay for dinner. We hugged and kissed our kids goodbye and walked to the car.

Phoenix opened my door for me, but I didn't get in. Instead, I turned into him and placed my hands on his chest. "Earlier, you said you blew up Octavius's house. Um, there's another building...the one where Ember and Coal were born, and Nathan, too. Uh, could we go see if it's still there?"

Phoenix cleared his throat and nodded. "Sure. Do you remember where it was?"

Oh, I would never forget where that damn building was. "Yes, I do," I answered, trying to keep the nerves out of my voice and gave him the directions.

He pulled up in front of the building that held so many bad memories for me. He sat silently beside me, holding my hand, while memories I did not cherish flooded my mind. "Is it being used for anything now?" I asked.

"No, doll face, it's empty."

"I swore if I ever had the chance, I would burn this damn building to the ground," I confessed.

"If you want to torch it, baby, I'll gladly hand you a can of gas and some matches," Phoenix said, pulling me into his arms.

"I know it won't change anything, but I really want to do it. I think I need to."

"Okay, let's do it," he said, reaching for his phone.

Minutes later, Dash arrived with a red jug full of gasoline and a box of long-reach matches. He wordlessly handed the items to Phoenix, nodded, and drove away in his truck.

"Before you get upset, I want you to know I called Dash because he truly understands how much Octavius took from our family. He is in love with our daughter and has felt every ounce of her pain. He was the one who ultimately captured Octavius and brought him back to the clubhouse. Then, he turned right around and saved my life. If anyone outside of our family gets it, it's him," Phoenix explained.

"No, he's probably wondering if he should marry a girl whose parents like to blow up and burn down buildings," I teased, trying to lighten the moment.

Phoenix chuckled. "Oh, he knew what he was getting himself into when Ember laid his ass out in the forecourt the day she showed up at the clubhouse."

"She did what?" I gasped.

"I'll tell you the whole story later. This building ain't going to burn itself."

"I don't know what I'm doing, Phoenix."

"Just pour the gas around the edges of the building. You can pour some inside if you want to. It's an old building, so when you're ready to light it, it should go up pretty quick."

I followed his instructions and dumped gas all around the outside of the building, but I had no interest in going inside. When the can was empty, Phoenix handed me the matches. "Strike it, drop it, and get back. Okay, baby?"

"Got it." It took me a minute to get the match lit with the way my hand was shaking, but I finally did it. I tossed the lit match at the base of the structure and quickly stepped back. When the flame made contact with the gas, the fire blazed to life with a loud whoosh.

Phoenix's arms circled my waist, and he pulled me back against his chest. We watched in silence as the place that held so many heart-wrenching memories for me burned to the ground.

I didn't even realize I was crying until Phoenix turned me by my shoulders and gently wiped the tears from my face. "Come on, doll face. Let's go home."

"Thank you," I whispered.

"Baby, if burning a building down makes you happy, I'll set the world on fire for you."

CHAPTER TWENTY-NINE

Phoenix

"Ember said things went well this morning. How were things with Coal?"

Annabelle smiled wistfully. "They were great. The time passed faster than I expected. They're both great kids, aren't they?"

I pulled her into my arms. "Yeah, doll face, they are." We stood there, in each other's arms for a long while. I had no intention of moving, but she asked a question that made my blood turn to ice.

"What happened to my parents?"

Fuck me. I sighed heavily. "Sit down." She made a face at me but took a seat on the couch. I dropped down beside her and ran my hand over my face. "I don't know what happened to them."

"What do you mean?"

"Exactly that. I don't know. I can't find any records of them having ever worked on the farm, legally or illegally. Much the same as you, they just disappeared." Octavius kept meticulous records of everything related to himself or the farm, especially the people he had working for him. My brothers and I had been through nearly all the papers and files. We'd yet to find a thing on the Burnetts, and I didn't think we would in the remaining files.

"Obviously, I didn't just disappear, and neither did they. Not that I give a shit about them, I just wanted to know if they were still around this area so I could avoid them while I'm here."

"If they are around here, I haven't run into them since I've been back in Croftridge. When I returned after my first deployment, I couldn't find them. I'll be honest and tell you I didn't spend a lot of time looking for them between learning of your disappearance and inheriting the farm. I have looked for them over the last year, but my most of my efforts were focused on finding you, not them," I explained.

She stayed quiet, but I could tell she wanted to

ask me something. "Just spit it out, Annabelle."

"You said Aaron was still around, right?"

"Yeah," I answered cautiously, wondering why she was asking about my VP. "Why?"

"Could you ask him to check out my old house? Just to make sure they aren't there."

"No problem, doll face. I'll give him a call right now." Her asking for Aaron made more sense. She didn't like people knowing where she lived back then, and I guess she still didn't. Aaron, Macy, and I were her only friends that knew where her house was.

Badger was more than happy to ride out to Annabelle's old house and take a look around. I knew her parents were worthless and she never liked them, but she almost seemed frightened of them. "Annabelle, are you scared of your parents?"

"Of course not. I just don't want to see them. Surely you can understand that," she replied. I would have believed her if she hadn't said it faster than normal and an octave too high.

"Try again," I growled.

She sighed. "It's not that I'm scared of them, I just don't trust them. They are toxic people, always have been. I don't want them in my life and I damn sure don't want them around my children."

"I get it. Now that I've found you, I'll put more focus on locating them. We'll go from there, okay?" I asked.

"Thank you, Phoenix. I really appreciate everything you've done for me and for our children," she murmured.

She didn't get it. I loved her. I never stopped loving her. Not for one second. Yeah, there had been other women over the years, but they were nothing more than a means to an end. I hadn't kissed another woman since the first time my lips met hers back in high school. Maybe it was time I told her how I felt.

"You don't have to thank me, doll face. I would do anything for you. You should know that."

She fidgeted with her hands and kept her eyes on the floor. "Annabelle," I commanded, "look at me." Slowly, she raised her head and brought her eyes to mine. "I love you. I never stopped and I never will."

I don't know what kind of reaction I expected from her, but it wasn't the one I got. She launched off the couch and crash-landed into me. She grabbed my face and stared right into my eyes, "I love you, too," she confessed and then she slammed her mouth down over mine.

I cupped her ass in my hands and stood, carrying her upstairs to my bedroom. Entering my room, I kicked the door closed behind me and didn't break my stride until I was placing her on my bed.

Without a word, I kept my eyes on hers while I removed her clothing, followed by my own. I crawled onto the bed, covering her body with mine and gently captured her lips.

Not a word was spoken between the two of us as I took my time and made slow, sweet love to the woman who captured my heart when I was 17 years old. When our lips weren't locked, our eyes were. We held each other in a tight embrace as our bodies moved together in perfect synchronization until we found our releases together.

***

Badger returned my call later that night. "I went by the house her parents lived in, and no one was there. It doesn't look like anyone has been there for years. The place is completely run down and ought to be condemned if you asked me."

"Thanks, brother, I appreciate it," I replied.

"May I ask why you had me ride out there?" he asked.

"Annabelle asked me if I knew where her parents were. I have no idea where they are or if they're dead or alive. I told her I would have someone ride by the house and she specifically asked if you would do it. I don't think she wants anyone who doesn't already know what pieces of shit they were to know anything about them."

"Makes sense," he said. "Why's she looking for them?"

"She's not. She just wanted to know if they were still around town so she could avoid them," I explained.

"Gotcha. Well, I'll swing by a few more times over the next week or so and make sure I don't see anything suspicious, but I highly doubt anyone is living in that place."

"Thanks, man."

Well, fuck. A part of me was hoping they might have gone back to that old shithole of a house and another part of me was hoping they were long gone, be it somewhere far away or somewhere six feet below.

"He didn't find anything, did he?" Annabelle asked.

"Woman," I hissed. "Don't sneak up on me like

that. You should know better than to eavesdrop on my conversations." She just stared at me, anxiously awaiting the answer to her question and not intimidated in the least. "No, doll face, he didn't find anything. We'll keep looking though."

Over the next few days, I continued to try to find something on the whereabouts of Annabelle's parents, anything. I was getting frustrated because every avenue I took led to a dead end. Finally, I sucked it up and called Luke for help.

He never acted like he minded helping me out from time to time, but I hated asking him. I knew he was a busy man with much bigger fish to fry, but my valiant efforts had failed. He readily agreed to help, assuring me it was no problem. I gave him all of the information I had on her parents. We talked for several minutes, and he said he would get back to me within a few days.

With that out of the way, I made my way to the common room to make sure everything was on track for the party that night. We had parties often, but this was the first one Annabelle would be attending, and I wanted everything to be perfect.

Annabelle showed up at the clubhouse a few hours later looking like sex on a stick. She had on a tight halter top that did the most wonderful things to her tits. Her shorts though, those were going to be the death of me. They were too fucking short, and she looked absolutely edible in them.

The guys noticed her immediately, and the room erupted in cheers. For a brief moment, I was afraid she was going to bolt, but she didn't. She smiled and sauntered in like she owned the place, walking straight to me.

"Hey, doll face," I said when she got near. I pulled her close for a very inappropriate kiss, her words, not mine. I didn't give a fuck where we were or who was watching. If I wanted to kiss her like I was about to fuck her, I was going to do it.

"Daddy! Your kids are here!" Ember whisper-yelled at me.

I laughed. "You do realize we had sex to create you, right?"

She hunched over like she was going to be sick and groaned. "Oh, please, someone make him stop before I puke all over the place."

Annabelle slapped her hand playfully against my chest. "Nix, behave yourself."

"Yes, ma'am," I replied. I would do anything for her, and she knew it.

I placed my beer on the bar and whistled loudly through my fingers to get everyone's attention. "I'm sure all of you know by now, but in case some of you missed it, this is my Annabelle."

The room erupted in cheers again, and the brothers immediately lined up to greet her and introduce themselves. She shared a warm hug with Badger and a tearful embrace with Patch while she thanked him for his help all those years ago. I wasn't crazy about them touching her, but I managed to keep my possessive tendencies under control.

The party was in full swing, and everyone was having a great time. The music was blaring. Annabelle and Ember were dancing on the makeshift dance floor with Reese, Harper, and some of the other girls. I was playing pool with Badger, Dash, and Duke in the common room while watching my sexy as hell Annabelle shake her ass.

"We win again," Dash proudly announced.

"Yeah, it'd be a different story if I had a partner that wasn't so damn distracted," Badger teased.

"Hey, Phoenix," Crystal purred into my ear, dragging her hand down my chest. "I bet I can hold your attention. Want to play with me and see?"

I flicked her hand away from my chest. "No, thanks. I've got a woman."

She moved back in, seeming to get herself even closer to me. "Get rid of her," she whispered in my ear while rubbing her fake tits on my arm. I was raising my hands to shove her away from me when a shrill screech came from Crystal as she was pulled away.

"You keep your motherfucking nasty ass whore hands off my man," Annabelle yelled into Crystal's face. She had a handful of her hair and was shaking her head with each word.

Crystal tried unsuccessfully to get out of my woman's grip. She straightened herself as best she could and demanded, "Who the fuck are you, bitch?"

Annabelle smiled an evil smile. "The correct response was 'I will.'" Annabelle then slapped her hand back and forth across her face while yelling, "He is mine, not yours. Don't touch."

"He isn't yours. He has an Old Lady," Crystal spat. Annabelle gasped and tossed Crystal to the floor, turning her furious eyes to me.

Shit.

Shit.

Shit.

"You have an Old Lady?" Annabelle screeched

in a tone that had Chop whimpering.

Well, fuck me. I wanted to tell her in private, so I could explain, but that option was blown out the window by a whore's breath.

"It's you," I said quietly.

She blinked, taken aback by my words. "Excuse me?"

"It's you. Claimed you the day I received my patch. I knew back then I would never want anyone else but you. Plus, if you did ever come back to Croftridge, you would have the club's protection, even if something happened to me," I explained.

"Why didn't you tell me?" she asked, her tone much calmer.

"I wasn't sure how you'd take it, especially with everything else going on. Figured you knew what it meant to be an Old Lady, particularly the president's Old Lady since you've been hanging with the Knights."

I turned to look at Crystal still sprawled on the floor, "This is my Old Lady, Annabelle. You know the rules." I arched my eyebrow and waited for her to spew more of her bullshit.

She surprised me and did what she was supposed to. "My apologies, Annabelle. I didn't know who you were."

"It's probably best if you head on out for the night," I informed Crystal.

"Yeah, sure thing." She rose to her feet, said something to one of the other club whores, and left.

Annabelle gave me a hard look. "We'll talk about this later. I'm going to go dance with the girls. Should I pee on your leg before I go?"

The guys laughed hysterically. I did my best to ignore them and cleared my throat to hide my own amusement. "I don't think that will be necessary."

CHAPTER THIRTY

Annabelle

After the party, Phoenix and I discussed the Old Lady thing. I knew it was the equivalent of a marriage in most biker clubs. I also knew that once a woman was claimed in front of the club, she couldn't do anything about it unless her Old Man unclaimed her. I wasn't sure if once unclaimed, one could be reclaimed. Not that it mattered, Phoenix would never do that. He had claimed me, I was his Old Lady, and there was nothing I could do about it, not that I wanted to.

The next morning, I had to get up while it was still dark outside, which was rather difficult given the party the night before. I had an early flight to L.A. to catch. I knew Nathan's schedule was tight, but he said he would have some time for me over the weekend. After Ember confessed that she really wanted Nathan to be at her wedding, I made the decision to tell him the truth about our past. That was most definitely a conversation that had to happen in person.

Phoenix drove me to the airport and walked me as far as they would allow him to go. He hugged and kissed me, fawning all over me. "I love you, baby. Be safe. Call me when you land, okay?"

I smiled. "I love you, too. I promise to call when I land." I laughed, "You're acting like I'm going to be gone for weeks or months. I'll be back tomorrow night."

"Sorry, doll face. I'm just not ready to let you out of my sight again. The last time we were at an airport saying goodbye, I didn't see you for 20 years," he said sadly and squeezed me even tighter to his chest.

"Oh," I replied. I hadn't thought about it that way. Determined, I said, "Well, that won't happen this time. I'll be back tomorrow. I promise."

The flight to L.A. was uneventful, though I did manage to catch up on some missed sleep. When I landed, I was pleasantly surprised to see

Wave and Token waiting for me at the terminal. I was planning on taking a cab to Nathan's hotel. "What are you two doing here?"

"Good to see you, too, Tater tot," Wave said with a laugh.

I waved my hand dismissively. "Oh, shush it. You know I'm happy to see you. I was just surprised."

"Your man called and asked if we could pick you up at the airport. He sounded a little worried, and we didn't have anything going on, so here we are. You ready to go?" Wave asked.

"Yep. I'm just staying the night, so I've got everything I need in my backpack," I answered.

On the drive to the hotel, I learned that Phoenix had not only asked Wave and Token to pick me up from the airport, he asked them to stay at the same hotel and return me to the airport the next day. Basically, he arranged 24-hour personal security for me. I wasn't sure if I should be angry or flattered.

I also decided that Wave and Token needed to know what I was going to tell Nathan so they could be there for him if he didn't take the news well. They were strong male figures in his life, and he may need to talk to someone after this had time to sink in.

I kept the story short and to the point. I didn't go into details about my feelings and all the other crap that went along with the worst period of my life. I just told them the facts of the past.

"You flew out here to tell him what you just told us?" Token asked. I nodded my head. "I'm going to make a suggestion. Maybe a little less robot and a little more human when you tell him that sordid tale you just shared."

I felt my cheeks heat. "Sorry, I was trying to keep my emotions out of it."

"I get that, but he's going to need to see the emotions to understand."

We arrived at the hotel and checked into our rooms. I wasn't the least bit surprised to learn my room, as well as theirs, had already been paid for and were located side by side. I shook my head. That man needed to learn some boundaries, but I couldn't blame him. Honestly, I didn't like being away from him either. If having Wave and Token nearby eased his worries, I had no problem with it.

After getting settled, I picked up my phone to send a text to Nathan when it started ringing in my hand. Phoenix's name flashed on my screen. Crap. I forgot to call him.

"Hey, Nix. Sorry, I forgot to call when I landed.

Everything is fine. I was just shocked to see Wave and Token waiting for me," I rushed out.

"I was worried, doll face," he rumbled.

"I know, and I'm really sorry. If you had told me you were having them meet me there, it wouldn't have thrown me for a loop, and I wouldn't have forgotten to call you," I retorted.

He barked a laugh. "Doesn't change the fact that I'm going to redden your ass when you get home for this."

"All right, hornball, I just got here, and I need to talk to Nathan. I love you, but I really don't have time for this right now."

"It'll be fine, Annabelle. He loves you, and he'll understand. Just be honest with him."

We said our goodbyes and I sent a text to Nathan to let him know I had arrived and what room I was staying in. He knocked on the door a few minutes later.

"Mom!" he exclaimed while picking me up and swinging me around.

"Holy crap, Nathan! You've gotten so much bigger in just a few short weeks. How is that even possible?"

He chuckled. "It's very possible when you spend all day five days a week working out and training. Now, you want to tell me what you're really doing here? It's not like you to schedule a trip at the last minute."

"You're right. I do have a reason for coming out without much notice. Um, are you free all afternoon? This is probably going to take a while."

"I'm free all day today and tomorrow," he replied.

The room I was staying in had a little sitting area when you first entered. I led him over to the sofa and gestured for him to sit while I remained standing. I knew I would need to pace as I got farther along in the story. I didn't waste any time beating around the bush. I launched right into the story, starting with Phoenix.

I told him everything. It took several hours to get through the entire story. There was yelling, crying, long periods of silence, and ultimately, forgiveness and acceptance.

"I understand why you did it, I really do. Mom, please don't be so upset," Nathan pleaded with me.

"I'm not crying because I'm upset, sweetheart. You have no idea what a relief it is to finally have it all out in the open. I hated lying to you. I thought about it every day, but I didn't have a choice. I had to protect you from that evil bastard," I explained.

"Mom, I'm glad you lied to me. I don't know how I would've handled it if I had known when I was younger. I could've grown up with an unfounded anger against you, or I could've grown up scared and always looking over my shoulder. Instead, I grew up happy, always feeling safe and secure," he said.

Despite who his biological father was, my son was a good man. I was so incredibly proud of him and the way he was handling this information. "So what made you decide to tell me now?"

I cleared my throat. "Your sister. That sounds weird, doesn't it? Anyway, your sister is getting married in two weeks, and she really wants you to be there. She waited to have the wedding until they found me. Now that she knows about you, she said she would postpone it again so you could be there."

"In two weeks? I'll still be at training camp," he explained.

"I know. Do you think you could fly out Friday night or Saturday morning and fly back on Sunday? Like I did this weekend?" I asked, hoping his answer would be favorable.

"I don't know. We have the weekends free, but the trainers didn't say anything in regards to leaving the area. Most of us are too damn tired to get out of bed on the weekends. I'll have to ask."

"Not to be pushy, but can you do that now? Ember and Coal want us to video chat with them this evening. I was hoping we would be able to tell Ember one way or the other about your attendance during the call."

Nathan nodded and placed a call to whoever was in charge and explained the situation. He was told that, normally, the team members had to stay in the city during the day and were to be back at the hotel at night on the weekends. Since this was a special circumstance, he granted Nathan permission to fly out Friday evening after practice. He had to be back by Sunday evening.

With that settled, we placed a video call to Ember. She was in her office at the farm, with Coal sitting right beside her. "Hey, Mom. Is he there?" she asked excitedly.

"Yes, he is. I'm going to set my phone on the table so you can see both of us. Just a sec." I fiddled with my phone until Nathan and I were both visible on the screen. "Okay, can you see us?"

Ember was bouncing in her chair. "Yes! Hi! I'm your sister, Ember, and this is our brother,

Coal. We're so happy to meet you!"

Nathan laughed. "Hi, I'm Nathan. It's nice to meet both of you, too."

We were all silent for a moment, then Coal spoke, "So this is a weird way to meet your siblings, right?"

After that, the conversation flowed. At one point, Phoenix came in and joined the conversation. I wasn't sure how Nathan would take his presence. I didn't want him to feel like he was an outsider in our little family, much the way I did when I first met Ember and Coal. Leave it to me to worry about nothing.

"So, Phoenix is the man you modeled my pretend father after?" Nathan asked while we were still talking to Ember, Coal, and Phoenix.

My cheeks were on fire. "Um, yeah, he is," I muttered.

"What was that?" Phoenix asked.

Nathan didn't hesitate to fill him in. "When I was younger and asked about my father, Mom told me he was a Marine, and he was killed during a deployment. She said her heart belonged to him and only him, which was why she never dated. She told me a lot of stories about my 'father,' and I just wondered if those stories were really about you."

Tears were streaming down my face. I covered my mouth with my hand to hold in the sob that wanted to escape. "Doll face, what's with the tears?" Phoenix asked.

Nathan turned to me. "Mom, what's wrong?"

I shook my head. The words were desperate to leave my mouth, but I didn't want to say them. Nathan put his arm around my shoulder and pulled me close. "Mom?"

"I wanted it to be him. He should have been your father. I love you with all my heart, but it should have been him," I sobbed into my son's shirt.

Nathan rubbed my back gently, trying to soothe me. After a few minutes he asked, "So, what, you want me to call him Daddy?"

I looked at my son like he was crazy and then threw my head back and laughed. Laughter from the three on the phone filled the room. My sweet boy, he always knew how to put a smile on my face.

We wrapped up the phone call, with me promising to call Phoenix later. When I told Nathan that Wave and Token were next door, he didn't hesitate to invite them over. After some hugs and chit-chat, we enjoyed a nice dinner out. I had missed Nathan a lot, as well as Wave and

Token. I made a mental note to thank Phoenix for having them tag along.

I met Nathan for an early breakfast the next morning. Then, he rode with Wave and Token to drop me off at the airport. After another tearful goodbye full of hugs and kisses, I was once again in the air.

CHAPTER THIRTY-ONE

Annabelle

The next morning, I realized I had some serious shopping to do. When I agreed to come home with Phoenix, I packed my bags with the essentials needed for two weeks. What I did not do was pack anything appropriate to wear to my daughter's bachelorette party, rehearsal dinner, and wedding.

Phoenix wasn't crazy about letting me out on my own, but he had too much work to catch up on with the club and the farm to come shopping with me. He did, however, assign two giant man-children to drive me to Cedar Valley and guard any shops I entered.

After scaring the pants off the little old

lady working in the first boutique I entered, I considered giving up and telling the guys to take me home. Before I could find the words, Prospect Kellan reassured me, "We're used to it, Annabelle. You go to whichever stores you want to and don't worry about us."

Well, okay then. The next store was much better. The staff was younger and seemed to be fascinated with the two bikers standing at the entrance. The clothes were much more my style, too. I grabbed a few dresses I liked and headed to the dressing room.

I liked the first dress I tried on, so I stepped out of the room to see how it looked in the 3-way mirror. I turned to get a look at the back of the dress and froze at the familiar voice. "Annabelle? Is it really you?"

I whirled back around and came face-to-face with Macy. "Hey, Macy," I said shyly and gave her an awkward little wave.

"Annabelle!" she shrieked and pulled me into a fierce hug. "What in the hell happened to you? The whole town was looking for you for over a year! Hell, I think some never stopped."

There was a loud commotion in the store and seconds later the dressing room was filled with two bikers ready to attack.

"Step away from Annabelle," Edge commanded, looking far more lethal than I ever thought he could with his baby face.

Macy held her hands up in the air like she was being held at gunpoint and backed away from me. She looked terrified. "Guys, it's okay. She's a friend from high school," I explained. When neither of them looked like they were going to relent, I continued, "She used to be Aaron's, I mean Badger's girlfriend."

Edge kept his eyes on Macy while Kellan stepped out of the dressing room, pulling his phone from his cut. Moments later he returned holding his phone in his hand. "Phoenix said it was okay to leave her in here with Annabelle," he said to Edge.

Edge nodded. "We'll be outside if you need us." With that, they went back to their original posts.

Macy was several feet away from me, still holding her hands in the air. "I'm sorry about that, Macy. Um, a lot of shit's happened, and Phoenix felt like I needed to have my own personal bodyguards while I was out shopping. They didn't know who you were," I tried to explain. When she continued to stare at me, I offered, "Would you like to go somewhere and talk?"

"Yeah," she said hoarsely, "I would really like that."

Forgetting about the dresses, Macy and I left the store and headed for the coffee shop on the corner. The guys sat a table far enough away to give us privacy while still being close enough to intervene if trouble came my way.

As soon as we had our drinks and were seated, Macy started, "So, what happened? I was supposed to pick you up from work one afternoon, but when I showed up at the shop, Phoenix's grandmother said you didn't show up that day, and they couldn't find you..."

"It's a long story. Do you have time to hear it?" I asked.

"I've wanted to know what happened to you since the day you disappeared. Even if I didn't have it, I would make the time to hear it."

So, I told her everything. Every single heartbreaking detail from the day I was taken to the farm to the day Phoenix found me in California. By the end of it, we had both shed more than our fair share of tears and had gone through two extra-large cups of coffee.

"Enough about me. Tell me about your life. Do you still live in Cedar Valley?" I asked, trying to change the subject to something lighter.

"Uh, I recently moved back in with my parents," she said, fidgeting with the napkin on the table. "I met a man when I was in college. He was from a wealthy family and had a good job, so I let him talk me into dropping out of college. I married him, and we moved to Texas." She paused and picked up another napkin to shred. "We just got divorced. So, here I am, 36 years old with no experience in the workforce and not a dime to my name, hence why I'm living with my parents," she said with a sniffle.

"Oh, Macy. I'm so sorry. Have you had any luck finding a job?" I asked.

She shook her head. "No, not yet. I was actually in that store trying to work up the nerve to ask if they were hiring. I'm not sure how many more rejections I can take."

I pushed to my feet. "Come on. I know a place that's hiring," I said, smiling proudly.

"You do?" she asked.

"I do. Let's go!" I ordered.

She followed me out to the SUV I was being carted around in and eyed the boys warily before climbing inside.

"Where to, Annabelle?" Edge asked from the driver's seat.

"We'd like to go visit Ember."

Macy and I continued to catch up during the 45-minute ride to the farm. Life had really done a number on her. She wasn't the same vibrant, live-in-the-moment girl she once was. Then again, I guess the same could be said about me.

I had to practically drag her to Ember's office. Knocking loudly, I waited a few seconds before pushing the door open and entering. I was still developing a relationship with Ember, and I didn't think walking in on her and her fiancé doing it on her desk would do either of us any good.

"Mom! What are you doing here? I thought Dad said you were out dress shopping," Ember said while crossing the room to hug me.

"I was, but I ran into a friend from high school while I was out." I pulled Macy, who was still in the hallway, into Ember's office. "Ember, this is my friend, Macy. Macy, this is my daughter, Ember."

"Hi, Macy. It's nice to meet you. Please, come in and have a seat," Ember said and gestured to the sofa in her office. "So, what brings you by, Mom?"

I smiled. "Well, I heard you mention you were looking for an office assistant, and Macy mentioned she was having trouble finding a decent job, and here we are."

Macy shifted in her seat and began explaining. "I'm a recently divorced housewife. I moved back to Cedar Valley to live with my parents while I get back on my feet. I don't have any job skills to speak of, but I did help organize a lot of charity functions and handled the donations received when I was married. I'm a quick learner and I'll—"

"Relax," Ember interrupted. "While the businesses and projects around the farm do operate at a profit, I started them because I wanted to help people. You sound like you need some help. If you want the job, it's yours. Oh, since we're located in the middle of nowhere, we provide our employees with a room on the property, sort of like a hotel suite."

Macy's jaw dropped, and she stared at Ember. I nudged her with my elbow and stage-whispered, "Say something."

Macy snapped her mouth closed and nodded. "Yes, I want the job."

"And the room?" Ember asked with an arched brow.

"Yes, please! I was seriously considering living in a cardboard box down by the Red River Bridge just to get away from my mother."

Ember chuckled and walked behind her desk. She pulled out a huge binder and started flipping through pages. "Ah, here we go." She jotted something in the book and pulled a key from her desk drawer. She held it out to Macy. "This is the key to your room. Take the next few days to move in and get settled. Be here at 8:00 am Monday morning. We'll get your papers filled out, and then you can get started. Does that sound okay?"

Macy got to her feet and hugged Ember. "It sounds wonderful. Thank you so much."

Ember smiled. "You're very welcome. Edge or Kellan can show you and Mom where your room is. I would, but I've got to get down to the barn to check on our newest employee and make Duke isn't trying to scare her off like he's done to the last three."

"Thanks, again," Macy said.

I hugged my daughter, so very proud of her. "Thanks, sweetie. Are you and Dash coming over for dinner?"

"Not tonight. He said he had something to do at the club, so Reese and I made plans to pig out and binge-watch Grey's Anatomy on Netflix."

"Okay, you girls have fun."

Edge and Kellan drove us over to Macy's new

building. I still wasn't completely comfortable being on the farm property, but it got a little easier each time. We took the elevator to the third floor and found her room at the end of the hall. Macy opened the door and gasped. "Annabelle, look at this place! This isn't a room. It's a freaking apartment!"

I shoved Macy out of the way and stepped inside to get a better look. She was right. We were standing in what appeared to be a two bedroom apartment. Make that a furnished two bedroom apartment. We went through the place, oohing and aahing over every little thing. It was far nicer than anything I had ever seen on the farm when I lived there.

When we were finished oohing and aahing over the apartment, the boys drove us back to Cedar Valley. Macy had left her car parked there, and I needed to finish dress shopping, even though it was the last thing I wanted to do.

"As a thank you for your help today, I'm going to help you finish shopping. Unless something has drastically changed, I'm guessing you still hate clothes shopping," Macy said.

"You are most certainly correct. I don't know what it is, but I just hate it, especially when it's for a special event. The whole thing stresses me out."

She giggled. "You just relax, and I'll have you fixed up in less than an hour."

She wasn't kidding. Less than an hour later, I was waving goodbye to her and climbing into the SUV with three dresses, three pairs of shoes, and accessories for each.

Phoenix was at the clubhouse and asked the boys to bring me there instead of taking me back to his house. I chuckled to myself about our obsessive need to see each other as often as possible. I was planning on asking them to swing by the clubhouse, so I could see him before going to the house.

He stood and came around his desk to greet me with a kiss when I walked into his office. A long, mouth-watering, panty-melting kiss. "Hey, doll face, how was shopping?"

"Huh?" I dumbly asked, still reeling from his magical lips.

He laughed and arched a brow. "Shopping? Did you find a dress?"

"Oh, yes, I did. Well, I didn't so much as Macy did, but that's neither here nor there. I have three dresses and all the shit I need to go with them."

He leaned against the edge of his desk. "Tell

me about Macy."

"Not a lot to tell. I ran into her in the dressing room. We talked over coffee. She's recently divorced. She moved backed to Cedar Valley and was living with her parents, but Ember hired her, and she's moving into one of the rooms on the farm property tonight."

"What?"

"Uh, she was having a hard time finding a job, and I knew Ember was looking for some help. It seemed like a win-win situation," I explained, not liking the sudden tension in the room.

"It probably is for Ember and Macy, but I don't know how Badger will feel about it."

"Why would it matter how he feels about it?"

"Badger and Macy didn't exactly part ways on friendly terms. She crushed him, Annabelle. I mean, she really did a number on him. I know it's been years, but I don't think he'll be happy to see her."

"What happened between them?" I asked.

"I have no idea. He didn't want to talk about it after it happened, and he never did."

"Phoenix, he was probably just butt-hurt about being dumped. If he never said anything else about her, he's probably been over it for a long time."

"Yeah, you're probably right. I've got a few things to finish up here. Do you want to stay and wait for me or go on to the house?"

"I'll see you at the house. I want to hang my dresses before they get wrinkled." I raised up on my tiptoes to give him a kiss before I left him in his office.

As I was putting my new dresses and accessories away, I decided I would drop by to check on Macy the following morning. Phoenix may not have been able to get Badger to talk, but I knew I could get Macy to tell me what happened. Besides, they were going to have to see each other sooner rather than later, seeing as how I already invited her to the wedding.

The phone ringing interrupted my thoughts. "Hello," I answered distractedly.

"Doll face, is everything okay?" Phoenix asked, sounding tense.

"Everything's fine. Is everything okay with you? I just left there."

"Yeah, I know. I need you to come back over to the clubhouse. I was just calling to let you know I was sending Coal to bring you over."

"Okay...you know I could've just walked over."

"Humor me, okay? I'll see you in a few." With that, he disconnected the call, leaving me with an uneasy feeling.

Coal and I walked to the clubhouse, and if my son knew why I was being summoned, he didn't let it show. He led me to Phoenix's office, kissed me on the cheek, and disappeared down the hall.

Anxious to know what was up, I pushed the door open and stopped dead in my tracks when my eyes landed on a face I'd never seen before, but instantly recognized because he looked just like his sister. "Luke," I whispered as tears welled in my eyes.

"Hello, Annabelle," he said with a soft smile. "It's nice to officially meet you." He stood and extended his hand to me.

I pushed his hand away and pulled him in for a hug. The man saved my son and me from a horrible existence; a handshake wasn't even on the table. "I never had the chance to thank you for everything you did for Nathan and me."

He returned my embrace, despite the low rumble coming from Phoenix. "I was happy to help, but now, I wish I'd known more about your situation. If I did, I could have—"

"Don't. If I've learned anything through this entire experience, it's that the 'what if' game does more harm than good. You did what you thought was the right thing at the time, and I will forever be grateful for your help," I told him honestly.

Phoenix tugged me away from Luke and held me against his chest like a damn caveman. Luke snorted, and I giggled. I tilted my head back to look at Phoenix. "Is this why you called me over here?"

He grimaced. "No, it's not. Luke has some information to share." Phoenix sat in the chair behind his desk and placed me on his lap.

"What information?"

Luke leaned forward in his chair and clasped his hands together. "Phoenix asked me for help tracking down your parents. I haven't been able to find anything on your father, but I may have something on your mother. Both of your parents went off the grid approximately 20 years ago, consistent with the time they would have started working off their debt with Octavius. Later that year, a significantly decomposed female body was found in a field on the outskirts of Croftridge. Efforts were made, but the body was never identified. It's possible the body belongs to your mother. Would you be willing to provide a DNA sample for analysis?"

"Uh, sure, I think. I mean, how would that work exactly? For all intents and purposes, I'm

Taylor Davis, not Annabelle Burnett."

"Right, but your DNA is still your DNA. I can run the analysis under the radar if you prefer. I don't mean to sound insensitive, but this would basically be just for your knowledge. The body has long since been buried or cremated," Luke explained.

"How did she die?" I asked.

"The medical examiner's findings were inconclusive due to the advanced decomposition. I'll spare you the details, but the report suggested she may have been beaten and died from her injuries, or it could have been from a drug overdose. There were drugs in her system, but the technology at the time couldn't produce accurate results based on the age and state of the tissue samples."

"Okay, I'll do it if you can keep it under the radar," I finally decided.

CHAPTER THIRTY-TWO

Annabelle

The day after Luke's visit to the clubhouse, Kathleen showed up to Phoenix's house for a surprise visit. She immediately pulled me into her arms, and we both burst into tears.

"Oh, my sweet friend, I've thought about you often over the years," she said.

"Same here. I don't even want to know what my life would've been like if it weren't for you," I confessed.

She waved her hand dismissively. "That was all you, sweetheart. I didn't do anything other than call my brother and drive you to the hospital."

I smiled at her modesty. "We'll have to agree

to disagree on that."

Phoenix entered the room to tell me he would be in his office at the clubhouse for most of the day. "Before you go," Kathleen said as she stood and whispered something in Phoenix's ear.

He smiled and nodded before walking out the front door. Kathleen turned back to me. "Just wait."

Moments later, Phoenix reentered the house carrying two large boxes. He placed them on the floor by Kathleen's feet, kissed me on the cheek, and left for the office.

Kathleen opened the box on top and said, "I know I shouldn't have, but I kept the things you brought over the day you left." She removed a much smaller box and handed it to me. "I never opened it, so if this isn't a welcome surprise, I'll take it back and never mention it again."

I shook my head and fought back the tears. "It's very welcome. Thank you," I whispered.

She reached out and patted my hand. "If you want to save that one for later, it won't hurt my feelings any."

I sniffled and nodded. "If you don't mind, I would like to look through it with Phoenix. It's full of mementos and things from the year we were together," I explained.

"I completely understand. There's plenty more we can look through together, but let's finish with this box first."

I didn't understand what she meant until she carefully pulled my old Christmas tree from the box. "My tree," I gasped.

"I saw it when I unpacked the toys for Coal. Obviously, it was special to you, and I never could bring myself to throw out Christmas decorations. We put it up in Coal's bedroom every year. Even though none of us knew it at the time, a part of you was with him each Christmas."

Once again, I turned into a blubbering mess. "I can't tell you how much that means to me."

"You don't have to. As a mother, I already know."

She gave me some time to get myself together before she declared it time to open the second box. "I like to take pictures. A lot of pictures," she said as she pulled several books from the box. "Each one of these books represents a year of Coal's life. Around 10 years ago, I got a coupon to create a photo book online for free. After I did one, I was hooked. I went back and did one for each year of his life and continued to do one as each year passed. And since each book was saved in my order history, it was a piece of cake for me to go in and order a set for you, which I did last night. I ordered a set for Phoenix after we found out he was Coal's biological father and his set should be here this week," she explained as she handed the first book to me.

I was blown away by her thoughtfulness. Instead of being defensive or threatened by us, she was welcoming Phoenix and me with open arms. At a total loss for words, I focused on the pages before me and spent the next few hours watching my son grow from an adorable infant to a handsome young man.

"Now, I can't promise anything, but I made a few calls to some of the women who used to look after the children. Many of them were living on the property because of their husbands' misdeeds and took Ember up on her offer to provide housing and help them get back on their feet when the farm was raided last year. Anyway, I've asked all the ones I could get in touch with to look through their things and send me any pictures they have of Ember so I can put together a few books of her for you."

"Oh, Kathleen, I would love that. Thank you so, so much!" I cried.

"You're quite welcome," she said and settled back into the sofa. "Now, tell me about your life after you got out of Croftridge. Coal wouldn't tell me diddly-squat."

I laughed and said, "Let me get us some coffee, and I'll tell you everything." And for the rest of the day, I did just that.

Kathleen stayed until Phoenix returned from the clubhouse. We made plans to get together for lunch the following week before she went home to her family.

"Did you two have a fun day?" Phoenix asked over dinner.

"We did. She brought some things over for me that I want to show you when we're finished eating."

He gave me a funny look before he nodded and told me about his day.

After dinner, he made himself comfortable on the sofa while I slid the large box in front of him before taking a seat at his side.

"Okay, close your eyes," I told him.

"Why?" he asked.

I huffed with impatience. "Just do it."

After several rounds of bantering back and forth, he finally gave in and closed his eyes. I removed my tree from the box and placed it on the coffee table. "Okay, open your eyes."

He did, and his eyes widened immediately.

"How did Kathleen get your tree?"

"The day she helped me escape, I showed up at her house with a box of things that were special to me. I told her I couldn't bear to leave them with Octavius and asked her if she would take care of them for me. I meant for her to throw them away, but she hid them away in her house instead."

"There's more than the tree?" he asked.

I nodded and pulled out the smaller box. "This box is full of our memories, from our year together. I haven't opened it yet. I wanted to wait and do it together," I explained.

He lifted his arm and looked at me expectantly. "Get in here, woman. I want to see what's in that box."

I giggled and snuggled up next to him, placing the box in my lap. Taking in a deep breath, I slowly removed the lid and was immediately transported back in time. The box was full of notes, ticket stubs, pictures, greeting cards, trinkets, even my Homecoming queen sash was in it. We spent hours looking at each and every item and reliving the memories associated with each.

"I can't believe you kept all this stuff," Phoenix admitted.

"Technically, I didn't. Kathleen did," I pointed out.

"Well, I'm glad she did."

"Yeah, me, too," I agreed.

Phoenix held up one of the last pictures taken of us. "It was only a year, but we made it one hell of a year, didn't we, doll face?"

I smiled wistfully. "We sure did."

"Can I ask you something?"

"You just did."

He snorted at my smart remark. "What happened to the phoenix necklace and earrings I gave you?"

I grinned. "I was told I could only take what I had on me when I left, so I made sure to wear them that day. I have them locked away in a safe at my house in California. What about your drawing? Do you still have it?"

He chuckled. "You haven't noticed it?"

"Obviously not. Where is it?"

"It's in the bedroom," he said on a laugh. "Guess I've been doing something right."

CHAPTER THIRTY-THREE

Annabelle

I didn't have a chance to go over and check in with Macy like I'd planned because I ended up spending the rest of the week helping Ember with wedding plans and helping her friend, Reese, plan her bachelorette party. Ember made the wise decision to have the bachelorette party the weekend before the wedding, but that didn't leave Reese much time to get things arranged.

When Saturday rolled around, the party had turned into an all-day event. First, we met at Ember's house for a catered breakfast. The next several hours were spent at the spa getting anything from manicures/pedicures and massages to mud baths and full body waxes. I opted for a pedicure, facial, and body scrub. I planned to get my nails done before the wedding, but there was no way I would keep them intact for an entire week.

We had a late lunch after the spa and then went back to Ember's house to get ready for our night out. I thought it might make Ember uncomfortable to have her mother tag along, but she assured me, several times, that she wanted me to attend. With all the girls in the house, it took several hours for everyone to be ready to go. Unbelievably, we didn't have to wait for anyone when our ride showed up.

Reese arranged for a stretch SUV limousine to drive us to and from the bachelorette party. Since Croftridge was such a small town, we had to drive to a larger city nearby to find some bars/clubs that would be suitable for this type of party.

Once in the limo, drinks were poured and passed around. Reese then informed everyone she had some special accessories for Ember to wear, which were a sash declaring her a bride-to-be, a tiara with a small veil attached, and a candy necklace. My drink nearly came out of my nose when I realized the necklace was made of little candy penises.

Once Ember had donned her new accessories, Reese presented her with a checklist of things to complete before the night ended. "Now, I know what a lot of you are thinking. Those brutes we claim as our men would totally flip their shit if they found out we were talking to or touching anyone of the opposite sex. So, to keep the peace, this list requires none of those things." She smiled proudly and handed the list to Ember, who promptly groaned and slapped her hand over her face.

"Oh, I almost forgot," Reese exclaimed and reached into her purse. She held up what looked like two credit cards and squealed, "I got Byte to make us fake IDs!"

"You did what?" Ember asked. "I don't want him to get into any trouble."

Reese smirked. "He won't. Your dad okayed it, but just for tonight. We have to give them back tomorrow."

Ember turned her worried eyes to me. "I'm sure your dad only agreed because he knew I would be with you. Enjoy your night, baby girl."

One of the other girls chimed in, "Tell us what's on the list."

Ember lifted the paper and began reading. "It's your final fling before the ring. The party won't stop until you've completed all of your tasks. To ensure your success, alternate shots and tasks as you move through the list. Tasks—Dance on a bar or table, Sing one karaoke song, Blow your candy pecker whistle when all of your candy penises have been devoured (by people other than yourself), Drop a penis straw in the drinks of five people you don't know, Collect 10 condoms from people you don't know. Shots—Blowjob, Cockteaser, Sex on the Beach, Screaming Orgasm, The Dash."

"How am I supposed to complete this list without interacting with men? And what the hell is 'The Dash'?" Ember shrieked.

"Relax. Women can eat the candy from the necklace. I mean, I don't think men would do that anyway. As for the condoms, just ask a woman or have one ask a man for you," Reese explained.

"And 'The Dash'?"

Reese laughed. "Oh, that's a shot I found online. It's made from two liquors I've never heard of. Supposedly, it tastes like strawberry cream. Anyway, you'll have to do it at the first bar because Duke knows one of the bartenders there and he agreed to make the shot if we supplied the ingredients."

Ember grinned mischievously. "One day, Reese Walker, you will be getting married, and I will get you back for this."

By the time we arrived at the first stop, almost everyone in our group had downed at least two drinks. I was trying to go easy on the alcohol so at least one person in our group had a clear head. Being the bride's mother, as well as the oldest in attendance, I silently volunteered myself for the position.

At the first club, we danced for a while, and the girls had a few more drinks. Ember completed a few tasks on her list. The funniest one thus far was watching her try to take a shot that was piled high with whipped cream with no hands. It took her several tries, but she finally managed to get it all down without making too much of a mess. After an hour or so, we left and headed to our second destination.

It was at the second stop that I noticed him. A man I had seen at the first club was now at the second club. I tried not to make too much of it as it was likely just a coincidence, but something about it just didn't sit right with me. I decided I would keep it to myself for the time being and keep an eye on him. I made sure to remind the girls not to leave their drinks unattended and not to accept any drinks from strangers.

We stayed at the second club a little longer than we did the first. The man was looming in the background the entire time. When we left to go to our third stop, I suggested we take the limo. The girls thought this was a great idea because their feet were getting sore from dancing in their high heels. I didn't make the suggestion to provide mercy for their abused toes. I wanted to have our ride nearby in case we needed to leave quickly and I thought driving would make it harder for anyone to follow us. I felt like I was being paranoid for no reason, but I just couldn't let it go.

We had a table reserved for us at the third club. As soon as I sat down, I immediately scanned the area. When I didn't see the man from the previous clubs anywhere, I breathed a sigh of relief. The alcohol was catching up to a few of the girls, so I was very glad we reserved a table. I danced with Ember and Reese in between checking on the ones at the table.

I had just turned around to head back to the dance floor when I saw him. The same man, and he was staring right at me. My chest tightened with fear, and I froze for a brief second before I reacted. I needed to get the girls out of there, but I didn't know how to do it without causing alarm. Doing my best to remain calm and not draw unnecessary attention, I walked to the bathroom. Of course, there was a freaking line. Here's the thing about drunk women, they talk a lot, and they pee slow.

After several minutes of standing in almost the same exact spot, I pulled my phone out and sent a text to Phoenix.

Annabelle: I think we're being followed. What should I do?

Phoenix: You are being followed.

Annabelle: What??

Phoenix: Shaker and Carbon have been tailing you all night.

Annabelle: I'm not talking about them!!!

Phoenix: WTF doll face?

Annabelle: Idk. Get them in here please.

Phoenix: Ok. Hang on babe.

Phoenix: They're not answering. I'm heading out. You stay put and keep the girls together.

Annabelle: I don't want to scare them.

Phoenix: You think a man is following you. My boys are on duty and not answering their president. You get the girls and stay put. I'm on my way.

Shit. I hoped I was overreacting. I would much

rather be embarrassed about being paranoid than be right about one of us being in danger. Finding out that Shaker and Carbon weren't answering their phones didn't ease my worry at all.

Since I was only in line so I could call Phoenix without anyone knowing, I turned around to go gather up the girls and stopped dead in my tracks. My eyes had to be deceiving me. I couldn't really be seeing the unknown stalker man talking to Crystal.

Not wasting any time and not giving a shit about drawing attention, I walked as fast as I could to the dance floor. I grabbed Ember's arm and tugged, "I need you to come to the table with me. All of you. Now!"

"Mom, what's wrong?" Ember asked, eyes wide.

"I'll explain in a minute. Help me get everyone rounded up and back to the table. Stay in groups of three or more," I said, grabbing Sarah, Ember's employee, by the arm and dragging her with me.

With everyone back at our table, I dropped into a chair and explained, "I noticed a guy following us. He's been everywhere we've been tonight, and he's been staring. So, I sent a text to Phoenix about it. Come to find out, Shaker and Carbon have been shadowing us all night, or were supposed to be, but Phoenix can't get a hold of them. He told me to gather up everyone and stay put. He's on his way now."

I faced Ember. "I'm sorry, baby. I thought I was just being paranoid. I called your dad so he could talk me down without upsetting you all. I didn't want to ruin your party."

"You didn't ruin anything, Mom. You did the right thing," Ember replied.

Reese was sitting quietly, staring off into space, her face uncharacteristically blank. "Reese, honey, are you okay?" I asked.

Ember whispered, "You realize Carbon's her brother, right?"

"Oh, I'm not sure I knew that," I said. "Hey, did you see Crystal earlier?"

"No. You saw her?" Ember asked.

"I thought I did, but it might not have been her," I lied. I knew it was her. I would have written that off as a true coincidence if I hadn't seen her talking to stalker man.

Hands slid over my shoulders from behind, causing me to scream and jump out of my chair. "It's me, baby! I'm sorry, didn't mean to scare you."

Phoenix. He would make everything better. He would take care of everything and get us home safely. "I'm so glad you're here. Did you find Shaker and Carbon?"

He shook his head. "Not yet. Dash and Duke are looking for them. Where's this fucker that's been following you?"

When I looked up, he wasn't standing in the spot he had been in all night. My eyes wildly darted around the club trying to spot him. My finger shot out. "That's him. The man walking toward the back door!"

"Stay!" Phoenix ordered and took off after him. The man pushed open the back door and stepped through it. Phoenix was hot on his tail and probably would have caught him if Crystal hadn't stepped out of the bathroom and directly into Phoenix's path. Phoenix tried to push her out of the way, but she grabbed on to his arm, which resulted in him sort of dragging her with him. He finally managed to shake her off and pushed through the back door. When he came back in moments later, I knew he had lost him.

He stomped past Crystal, completely ignoring her, and returned to where we were seated. "I saw what happened," I told him before he even said anything. "I also saw her talking to that man earlier, right after I sent that text to you."

Without a single word, Phoenix turned around and stalked toward Crystal.

CHAPTER THIRTY-FOUR

Phoenix

"What the fuck are you doing here?" I asked Crystal.

She blinked her overly made up eyes at me, "I work here."

"You work here. Since when?"

She huffed. "Since I got into it with your Old Lady. I figured all it would take was one word from her, and I would be out on my ass. I started looking for a part-time job the next day."

"Who was the man you were talking to?"

"Could you be a little more specific? I'm a waitress in a bar. I talk to a lot of men," she sassed.

"Cut the shit. The man I was chasing out the

back door. The man you intentionally stopped me from chasing. Gray shirt, blue jeans, about 5'10, 180lbs. That guy," I barked. I didn't have time for her bullshit.

"I swear, Phoenix, I was just coming out of the bathroom. I didn't know you were chasing anybody. Wait, is everything okay? Why were you chasing him?" she asked.

"Club business," I barked. "What was the man's name?"

"I have no idea," she shrugged. "The man you described paid with cash all night."

Of course, he fucking did. "If I see him again, do you want me to get his name?" she offered.

"Sure. Whatever. Listen, I've got to get back," I said and stepped around her. I wasn't sure if she was lying to me or not, but either way, I doubted she would bring me a name.

I returned to the table to find Dash, Duke, Shaker, and Carbon with the girls. "Where the fuck have you two been?" I growled.

"Being hassled by bouncers and then the cops," Carbon spat.

"Somebody told the bouncer at the first club they saw us put something in a girl's drink. The bouncer called the police and was able to stall us long enough for them to arrive." Shaker shrugged. "Sorry, Prez, we couldn't answer our phones with cuffs on."

I pinched the bridge of my nose. I could feel a headache coming on. "Let's get the fuck out of here. We can discuss everything else back at the clubhouse."

***

After giving it some thought over the next few days, I couldn't convince myself one way or the other about the man at the club. It could have been a coincidence, or it could have been someone legitimately following them. The part that was troubling me was I didn't know who he was following and why. With little to go on, there wasn't much I could do other than tell the girls to be vigilant and travel in pairs.

I was also frustrated with the situation regarding Annabelle's parents. How could two fuck ups like them just disappear without a trace? It took skill to not be found. There was no way those two were capable of anything like that.

Finally, Luke called with the results from Annabelle's DNA sample. "Hey, Phoenix. Sorry, it took a little longer than I thought, but we got a match. The body belonged to Lisbeth Maynard Burnett."

"Yeah, I kinda had a feeling it did. Thanks for going to so much trouble for Annabelle. I know it will ease her mind to know what became of at least one of them. You find anything on her father, yet?"

"No, but I'll keep looking. About her mother... something's not sitting right with me. From what you told me, Octavius tried to use Annabelle's parents as a bargaining chip in order to get her to comply with his wishes, correct?"

"Yes, that's what he said, and she later confirmed it. What's that have to do with anything?"

"Well, an exact time of death couldn't be determined, but it was estimated to be three months prior to the body's discovery, meaning she died in August, the same month Annabelle and her family were taken to the farm. Octavius had to know she wasn't working on the farm. So, how did he plan to use her as a bargaining chip if she wasn't there?"

"Fuck me. You think Octavius killed her?"

"I honestly don't know, Phoenix. We never found any records of either of them working for him, and you said yourself he kept meticulous records. I try not to make guesses, but something about this feels off."

"Yeah, I agree with you on that. Fuck, I can't tell her this now. Our daughter is getting married tomorrow. Hell, we were supposed to leave for the rehearsal dinner 15 minutes ago."

"Go enjoy your weekend with your family. I'll keep the results to myself and you can tell her whenever you think is best."

"Thanks, Luke. Appreciate it."

I disconnected the call and wondered what in the hell we were about to uncover. Unfortunately, I didn't have the time to dwell on it. I had a weekend full of wedding festivities, starting with the rehearsal dinner. "Annabelle! Let's go! We're going to be late!"

"Almost ready," she called back. Yeah, that was the fourth or fifth time she'd said that. If she wasn't walking out the door in five minutes, I was going to leave her ass at home. I hated being late.

When I heard her heels clicking down the stairs, I looked up and lost the ability to breathe. She had on a strapless, red dress that hugged her curves and stopped just an inch or two above her knees. Her legs were bare, but she had on the sexiest pair of strappy high heel shoes. Oh yes, I would be balls deep in her later, and she would only be wearing those shoes.

"Phoenix, aren't you going to say anything?" she asked, clearly annoyed.

"Sorry, doll face. I needed a minute. You took my breath away when you came down the stairs. Damn you look good in that," I said, taking quick strides to her. I put my hands on her hips and pulled her to me. "I will be fucking you in those shoes later." She moaned and pressed her hips against mine. "If you don't stop that, I'll be fucking you before we go, too."

She gasped. "No, Phoenix. You'll mess up my hair."

That was her only protest? I growled, "I won't touch your fucking hair. Turn around and put your hands on the stairs."

"Phoenix, we don't have time for this," she protested, weakly.

I spun her around and pressed on her back, forcing her to bend forward and place her hands on the stairs. Pushing the hem of her dress up over her hips, I grabbed the minuscule piece of fabric she was trying to pass off as underwear and, with a quick tug, I tore her panties from her body, baring her wet pussy to my hungry eyes.

"Spread 'em wider for me, baby," I said as I

freed my cock from my pants. She widened her stance, and I stepped forward, rubbing the head of my cock through her slippery slit.

"You're soaked, baby. Were you wanting me to fuck you?"

"I always want you to fuck me," she moaned, trying to push herself back onto my cock.

I slapped her ass. "Bad girl. You get my cock when I give it to you."

"Please give it to me."

I grabbed her hips and shoved into her, setting a hard and fast pace. Reaching around with one hand, I rubbed her clit to help push her over the edge. Half a dozen more thrusts and I felt the walls of her pussy rippling around my dick while she clawed at the stairs and screamed my name. Seconds later I was shooting my own release into her.

We were a few minutes late to the rehearsal, which everyone pointed out because I am never late. Annabelle turned the color of her dress from head to toe, clearly giving away the reason for our tardiness. Once everyone had gotten their jabs in, we got down to business and knocked the rehearsal out in less than an hour.

The dinner was at a nice Italian restaurant in town. The only downside was Gram and Pop weren't there. Gram called a few hours before the dinner in a tizzy because their flight had been delayed. According to Gram, the small airport basically shut down because the President just had to visit his coastal home on the same weekend of her granddaughter's wedding. Gram continued to rant until Pop took the phone from her and explained they would be on their way as soon as the airspace restrictions were lifted. At least they weren't going to miss the wedding.

Surprisingly, we managed to have a nice, drama-free dinner. Afterward, Annabelle left with Ember and the girls, shadowed by Coal, Edge, and our newest prospect, Kellan, while the rest of the boys and I went back to the clubhouse.

It was a Friday night, so the brothers not in the wedding party already had the party going at the clubhouse. I wasn't planning on staying long. Annabelle was dropping the girls off and then going to the airport to pick up Nathan. I wanted to go with her, but she didn't want to overwhelm him right away. I didn't quite get that. He knew about me and his siblings, but she was his mother and knew what was best.

I leaned back against the bar and brought my beer to my lips. I noticed Crystal eyeing me, as she wriggled in the lap of another brother.

I didn't acknowledge her, just turned my head and continued my conversation with Badger. When I looked back several minutes later, she had her eyes on me again.

"She causing problems again?" Badger asked, nodding his head slightly in Crystal's direction.

"Nah, but I don't know why in the fuck she keeps looking at me."

"She wants you. She's letting you know," he said, like I was an idiot.

"I know that, fucknut. I've already made it clear to her that I'm not interested. She needs to let it go, or I'm going to have no choice but to kick her ass out."

"Might not be a bad thing. She's always been mouthy, and she ain't that great in bed."

"I'll have to take your word on that, brother," I laughed.

"You ain't fucked her?" he asked.

I shook my head. "Nope. Let her suck me off once when she first started coming around, but that's it. She begged me to fuck her, but it wasn't happening."

Badger let out a loud belly laugh. "Well, that explains a lot. No wonder she's staring you down. She wants a ride on the Phoenix."

I shoved him and laughed. "Shut the fuck up,

you idiot."

For a brief second, I considered telling him about Macy being back in town, but things were going smoothly for once, and I didn't want to ruin it. Bringing up Macy would do nothing but ruin his good mood. It would be better to tell him after the wedding.

I finally got fed up with Crystal's staring and went to my office. I was waiting for Annabelle to call me and let me know she had Nathan settled. She thought it would be best for him to stay at my house instead of the farm, but she didn't want me there when he arrived. She was being really weird about the whole thing with Nathan. I knew they had a fucked up history with this town, so I was trying not to press her about the way she was acting.

Just as I was starting to worry, she called. "Hey, doll face. I was starting to get worried about you. Everything okay?"

Her shaky voice filled my ear. "No Phoenix, it's not. Someone slashed my tires when I went inside to get Nathan."

"Where are you now?" I barked, grabbing my keys and heading for the door.

"We're back inside the airport, near the security office. I reported it, but they don't have cameras in that lot, so I doubt they'll be able to do anything. Can you come pick us up?"

"I'm already heading out the door. I'm bringing Badger with me. We'll arrange a tow on the way. You stay inside that airport until I get there."

"I will."

"Badger! You're with me. Let's go," I yelled, striding through the common room.

Dash jumped up from his place at the bar. "What's up, Prez?"

"Annabelle's at the airport, and she's got flat tires. Going to pick her and Nathan up," I said quickly, hoping he missed the part where I said tires instead of a tire.

"You coming back here tonight?" he asked.

"Just to drop Badger off, then I'll take them home."

He slapped me on the back. "All right, Prez, see you in the morning."

Badger and I climbed into one of the SUVs we kept out back. "What's really going on?" he asked.

"Annabelle's tires were slashed at the airport while she was inside getting Nathan. Call and find out where the fuck Edge is. He's supposed to be tailing her. And I need you to arrange a tow for the car," I said as I sped out of the lot in a spray of dust and gravel.

Just as Badger pulled his phone out, mine started ringing. I tossed it to him so I could concentrate on getting to my woman as fast as possible.

Badger answered and put the phone on speaker. "Prez, I lost Annabelle. A fucking car swerved and ran me off the road," Edge grunted into the phone.

"You okay, brother," Badger asked.

Edge coughed and cleared his throat. "Laid my bike down. I think I'm okay. Called as soon as I found my phone."

"Stay put. I'll have someone there to get you and your bike shortly. You sure you're okay?"

"I'm sure. I'm sorry, Prez."

"Ain't your fault, brother. She's at the airport, and she's okay, but someone slashed her tires while she was inside. We're going to get her now. You stay alert until I get another brother to you, you hear?" I ordered.

"Got it, Prez."

Well, fuck me. I made good time getting to the airport. Parking at the curb, I jumped out and went to find my woman. She must have been watching for me because she met me right inside the door, with Nathan at her side. He had gotten a lot bigger since the last time I saw him. I looked down at Annabelle. "You okay?"

"Yeah, we're fine. I'm just pissed that someone did that to your car. I'll pay to have it towed and for the repairs," she said.

"You will do no such thing. I brought Badger with me, and he's already arranged to have it towed back to the clubhouse tonight. Anything you need out of it before we go?" She shook her head. "All right, let's get you in the car and get back home."

I wasn't about to tell her what happened to Edge. Reason number one being she didn't know I had a tail on her. Reason number two, I didn't want her feeling as uneasy as I was.

CHAPTER THIRTY-FIVE

Phoenix

The day of the wedding was a whirlwind of activity. Ember wanted to have the wedding out by the lake on the clubhouse property. She arranged to have a tent set up by the lake for the reception. The gates were opening and closing from the crack of dawn with delivery after delivery of wedding shit. The girls were at Ember's house helping her get ready, and the brothers were helping out around the clubhouse to get things set up.

Pop and Gram arrived mid-morning. I was surprised that Gram didn't go over to the farm to help the girls, but she informed me that a woman needed to oversee the setup and decorations and she was that woman. Pop, of course, hung back with me. "What are you not telling me?" he asked. The man had an uncanny way of reading people.

I sighed. "I don't want to make a big deal of it, okay?" At his nod, I told him about the bachelorette party and Annabelle's tires being slashed. "On top of that, Luke's been helping me search for her parents. He mentioned an unidentified body found years ago as a possibility and Annabelle agreed to give a DNA sample for comparison. He called yesterday to tell me it was a match, but I haven't shared the news with Annabelle yet."

"Anything on her father?"

I shook my head. "Nothing yet. All of it's got me on edge. I've been keyed up since I found her, waiting for someone or something to take her away from me again, and I think that's clouding my judgment."

"It doesn't sound like it's clouding your judgment. You've not jumped to any conclusions or made any outrageous accusations. You're being cautious and waiting for more information. Sounds exactly like what you would be doing any other time," he said, patting me on the shoulder.

"Thanks, Pop. I needed to hear that."

Blessedly, the day progressed without incident. When it was time for the ceremony to begin, I waited outside the tent for Ember to exit with her bridesmaids. She was the last to step out, and my breath caught in my throat when I saw her. Her hair was curled and piled on top of her head in some fancy updo, but that was where the fancy ended. She had on very little makeup and was wearing a simple white dress. She looked like she should be running through a field of wildflowers.

"Dad?" she asked when I continued to stand there speechless.

I cleared my throat. "You're beautiful, baby girl," I whispered.

She shook her finger at me. "Not another word. If you make me cry, my eyes will be all red and puffy when I walk down the aisle, and that is not happening."

I laughed. "All right, let's get this show on the road."

We were poised at the end of the aisle, waiting for our cue to go, when she whispered, "Thanks, Dad, for finding Mom."

I walked Ember down the aisle and struggled to keep my emotions in check. My baby girl was a beautiful woman and an amazing person.

When we reached the altar, I turned to face her. Speaking quietly so only she could hear, I told her, "The day you showed up at the clubhouse was one of the best days of my life. Without your strength and determination, I wouldn't have you, your mother, and your brother in my life. There are no words to express how proud I am of you. I love you, baby girl."

I kissed her cheek and turned my eyes to Dash. Loud enough for everyone to hear, I made my obligatory fatherly threat. "Hurt my baby, and I'll cut your balls off before I kill you." Laughter erupted from the guests while I turned and took my seat.

Once again, I struggled to control my emotions when I caught sight of Annabelle. She had spent most of the day helping Ember and the bridesmaids get ready, so I hadn't seen her in several hours. She looked stunning in her champagne colored dress with black lace detail that fell just below her knees. And her shoes. She was killing me with the shoes. Shiny nude colored pumps with at least a five-inch heel. I sat down beside her and kissed her cheek as well as discretely nipping her ear before pulling back.

Wrapping my arm around her shoulders, she leaned into me as we watched our daughter marry the man she loved in front of her family and friends.

Once the ceremony was over and the guests were starting to head to the reception, Gram rushed to Annabelle and swept her into a huge hug. "Oh, Annabelle, my sweet girl! I was afraid I'd never see you again!"

"Mrs. Black!" Annabelle squealed and returned Gram's fierce embrace.

"Oh, none of that. You call me Gram, just like you did years ago." Gram let go of Annabelle and took a step back to study her. "Still as beautiful as you ever were." She grabbed Annabelle's wrist and started to pull her away. "Come with me, you and Phoenix are at our table. We've got a lot of catching up to do."

"Hang on a second there, love," Pop chimed in and pulled Annabelle into a hug. "I sure am glad you're back in these parts, sweetheart. Is this your youngest son?" he asked, nodding toward Nathan.

"Yes, sir. This is my son, Nathan Davis. Nathan, these are Phoenix's grandparents, Mr. and Mrs. Black."

Pop shook Nathan's hand while keeping one arm around Annabelle. "Pleased to meet you. Phoenix tells me you just signed a contract with an MMA league on the west coast. Your mom must be mighty proud of you."

"I hope so, sir," Nathan replied.

"Same goes for me, none of that formal crap. I'm Pop, and she's Gram. We are family after all," he declared, eliciting a shy smile from Nathan.

We made our way over to the tent housing the reception. I didn't participate in the wedding planning¬—other than handing over my credit card—so I wasn't expecting to see something that rivaled a damn hotel ballroom on the inside of a canvas tent in the middle of a field beside a motorcycle club's clubhouse.

The girls had gone all out. It wasn't my cup of tea, but the smiles on Annabelle's and Ember's faces made it worth it.

By the time the reception was over, everyone was either exhausted or drunk. Even Gram was on the far side of tipsy. Luckily, no one had to drive to get anywhere. My house was on the property. Gram, Pop, and Nathan were staying with me and Annabelle. Ember and Dash were going back to their house, but they had a limo taking them. Everyone else was staying at the clubhouse.

Nathan had to leave for the airport at 6:00 am the following morning. He insisted upon driving himself so his mother didn't have to get up and do it. Since we had to take Ember and Dash later that afternoon to catch their flight for their honeymoon, we could pick up the car Nathan drove then. With that settled, we all went to bed.

***

My phone woke me at 8:00 am the next morning. I had a bad feeling. No one would be calling me at this hour the day after my daughter's wedding unless something was wrong. Not even bothering to look at the phone, I answered, "Phoenix."

"Prez! Get to the clubhouse right now! He's gone!" Duke yelled down the line.

I shot up straight in bed. "Who?"

"Octavius!"

"Fuck! I'll be right there!" I disconnected and turned to wake Annabelle. Unfortunately, she was already awake and had obviously heard everything Duke said. She was on her feet and shaking, white as a ghost.

"I thought he was dead!" she shrieked.

"He is on paper. I can't explain right now. I've got to find him. I need you to get Gram and Pop over to the clubhouse. Can you do that for me?"

I asked, taking a step toward her.

She took a step back from me. Fuck, I didn't have time to reassure her, even though I wanted to. "Please, Annabelle," I pleaded, begging her with my eyes to understand the urgency of the situation.

"Fine," she huffed and stomped out of the room. Good, anger was better than sadness or fear.

I dressed quickly and ran the entire way to the clubhouse. Pushing through the front doors, I bellowed, "Somebody tell me what in the fuck is going on!"

Badger stepped forward. "Duke went down to take him his breakfast. He noticed the basement door wasn't locked, but went on down anyway. When he got down there, Octavius's cell was wide open, and he's nowhere to be found."

"Byte, does he still have that tracker?" I asked.

"As far as I know, Prez. Already on it," he said, typing away on his laptop. "Got him! Looks like he's at a warehouse up near the Disciples of Death's territory."

Before I could comment, Pop, Gram, and Annabelle came through the front doors. "What's going on, Phoenix?" Pop asked.

"I can't explain right now, Pop. I need you to

stay here and look after Gram and Annabelle for me."

"Whatever you need, my boy," Pop answered.

"Move this into Church, now!" I ordered.

Once we were behind closed doors, I shared my thoughts. "I don't think this requires much planning, brothers. I say we just drive out there and get him."

The boys started discussing whether or not we should do just that when my phone beeped in my pocket. I pulled it out to see I had a video message from an unknown number. I was pretty sure I could guess who the message was from.

I flipped my phone open and gaped at the image on the screen. Hesitantly pressing play, I watched in horror as Nathan, tied to a chair, was hit in the face repeatedly by someone's fist. A voice I didn't recognize began speaking, "If you want him back, you'll have to pay. I want $250,000 in cash. No cops, no brothers, no bullshit. You have four hours to gather the money and be ready. I'll text the instructions for drop off then."

I tossed my phone on the table and dropped my head into my hands. Who the fuck was talking in the video? How did they get Nathan? Where was Octavius? Was he a part of this or was it something separate? I couldn't think. I was losing it when I needed to keep it together the most.

Badger stood and clapped his hands together once. "Okay, brothers, this changes the game. I don't think it's a coincidence that Nathan, who is Octavius's biological son, was kidnapped the same day Octavius escaped. Looked to me like the background in the video was that of a warehouse. I'm guessing that's where Nathan is. What I don't know is who the other person in that video is..."

Badger trailed off when we heard a commotion on the other side of the door. Duke yanked the door open to see what was going on. Annabelle had Crystal on the ground and was laying into her with a ferocity I didn't know she was capable of. "I've already told you, you filthy cum dumpster. He is my man. MINE!" she screamed while landing punch after punch to Crystal's face.

I pulled Annabelle off Crystal. She fought like hell to get away from me and back to taking Crystal to task, but her struggles were useless. "Crystal," I barked, "get the fuck out of here and don't come back." She quickly got to her feet, shot me a scathing look, and stomped out the front door. "Prospect Kellan, follow her and report back where she goes."

I looked down at Annabelle. "You can explain that later. We've got to get back in Church."

At some point during the episode with Annabelle and Crystal, my mind had cleared, and I was back in full president mode. "Hold your thoughts for a moment. I'm going to call Copper and see if he can send a man or two out to scope out the warehouse and surrounding area. He's closer and can get someone there a lot faster than we can."

"You could give Boar a call. He's closer than Copper," Carbon, of all people, suggested.

"Good thinking, man. I'll call both."

Copper and Boar both readily agreed to help any way they could. Time was ticking by slowly, waiting to hear from anyone so we could decide our next move. I wanted to have a plan in place before Annabelle figured out that Nathan missed his plane.

"Phoenix," I barked into my phone.

"Prez, it's Kellan. I followed the girl like you said. She's at the Disciples of Death's clubhouse."

"You're fucking shitting me? All right, keep eyes on her, but don't let anybody spot you. Follow her if she leaves and report back."

"Will do, Prez."

I faced the brothers in the room. "Crystal is at the Disciples of Death's clubhouse."

Shouts of anger and disbelief sounded. We spent the next 30 minutes discussing possible scenarios and plans of action.

My phone rang again, Kellan's name appearing on the screen. "Prez, she left the clubhouse and now we're at some warehouse out in the middle of nowhere." He lowered his voice, "I've seen some other bikers around here. Not many, but they're skulking around like I am."

"Hang on a sec, Kellan," I spoke into the phone. "Hey, Badger, who did Copper send out to the warehouse?"

Badger chuckled. "Who do you think? Judge and Batta."

"Kellan, the bikers you saw, are they big bastards? One looks like Duke, and the other one looks like a mean Mr. Clean?" I asked.

"Yeah. Yeah, that's exactly what they look like."

"That's Judge and Batta, the SAA and enforcer from our Devil Springs chapter. We'll let them know you're there, too. Hang back and follow their orders like you would mine, understand?"

"Yes, Prez."

"All right, brothers, Crystal just showed up at the warehouse where Octavius is and likely Nathan, too. Not sure how the Disciples of Death play into this, but the other pieces are starting to fit together," I said.

Someone knocked on the door to Church, then immediately started banging on it. Duke jerked the door open again. Annabelle came tearing into the room, crying and shoving her phone in my face.

"What's wrong, doll face?" I asked, even though I already knew, or thought I did.

"Look at this! Look!" she yelled, shaking her phone at me.

I took it and pressed play on the video she had pulled up on her screen. It was the same one that was sent to me earlier. "I know, baby, it was sent to me, too. That's what we're working on in here. I was hoping we could get him back before you found out about it."

She huffed and stomped her foot. "I know all that. You don't recognize that voice?" I shook my head. "It's my fucking father!"

Once she said it, I did recognize his voice. Fucking hell. "How in the fuck did he get involved in this?" I asked, more to myself than anyone else.

Annabelle latched onto my arm and started shaking me. "It doesn't matter! Just go get my son back!"

"All right, baby," I pulled her to me and held her for just a moment. I needed the comfort as much as she did at that point. I placed a kiss on top of her head. "Go wait out there with Gram and Pop while we get our plan together, okay?" Surprisingly, she didn't argue and quickly left the room.

"I'm not sure how Annabelle's father plays into this, but I'm willing to bet he's in that warehouse with Octavius and Crystal, and Nathan. Anyone object to just riding in and taking them out?" I asked.

With no objections from the officers, we left Church and got ourselves ready to ride out. I touched base with Boar and Copper to let them know we were moving in to rescue Nathan. Copper said he would have Judge and Batta keep eyes on the place and he would call if there was any activity. Boar had two boys with eyes on the warehouse already but said he and some of his boys would ride out for back up if needed. Within 15 minutes, we were on the road.

CHAPTER THIRTY-SIX

Phoenix

I pulled into a parking lot roughly a mile from the warehouse. A few of Boar's members were already there waiting for us. Boar stepped out of a cage and walked over to my bike. "I just talked to Copper. No one has been in or out of the warehouse since Crystal arrived. Can't say for sure, but it doesn't sound like anybody is in there except the four of them."

"Thanks, man. Appreciate you helping us out like this," I said to Boar. I was surprised he actually came with his boys. He was still recovering from being shot during the same incident that injured Coal. His recovery was slower than Coal's due to the location he was shot and his age. Boar nodded in acknowledgment of my gratitude. We would probably owe him a marker for this, but I was okay with that.

"Here's how we're going to do this. We'll ride up some more and stop about a half mile from the warehouse. We'll leave the bikes and approach on foot. Once there, we'll split off into groups and surround the warehouse. Carbon and Shaker, once we breach, you two get Nathan out as fast as possible. The rest of you shoot to kill anyone in there except Octavius. I'll be the one to send that fucker to hell," I growled.

With that said, we rode to the half-mile point Byte mapped out for us and walked the rest of the way. We functioned like a well-oiled machine. Half the group went one way while the other half went in the opposite direction to surround the building. Badger and I inched along the side of the warehouse until we found a door that was stupidly ajar. I made eye contact with him and nodded. Holding my fist down by my side, I ticked off one, two, three with my fingers. On three, I eased the door open and stepped inside.

The door opened to a large room with concrete walls and floors. In the middle, Nathan was tied to a chair; his head slumped to his chest. Off to the side, Octavius and another man who I assumed was Annabelle's father since I couldn't see his face were in a heated argument. At their feet, Crystal's lifeless body lay in a pool of her own blood. Badger and I simultaneously raised our guns, took aim, and fired.

Octavius and the other man dropped to the ground. Annabelle's father didn't so much as twitch thanks to the bullet Badger lodged in his skull. Octavius, on the other hand, was rolling around on the ground, clutching his leg, and screeching like a banshee. I went straight for Octavius and quickly tied his hands behind his back.

Carbon and Shaker rushed in and began untying Nathan who was starting to come around. As they were carrying him out to the van, I heard Carbon mutter, "Well, that was anticlimactic." I shook my head. I wondered about that boy's sanity sometimes.

Boar strolled through the door and looked around the room before his eyes settled on Annabelle's father. "What in the hell did Gnaw have to do with this?"

"Who's Gnaw?" I asked distractedly. I was still hovering over Octavius, contemplating shoving a gag in his mouth. I was so grateful we had accomplished our goal without incident that

I hadn't bothered to take in any details of our surroundings.

Boar pointed to the man on the ground. "That fucker right there with the Disciples of Death cut on. He was a vicious son of a bitch."

"Fuck me! That's Annabelle's father. Fuck, this just keeps getting better. On top of everything else, now I've got another club to deal with." I pinched the bridge of my nose and shook my head. "I'm going to get this piece of shit secured and see how Nathan is. Then, we can start on the cleanup."

The rest of the guys followed me outside as I drug Octavius by his bound hands to a cage. I guess no one wanted to wait in a poorly ventilated warehouse with two dead bodies in the middle of a scorching summer. I shoved Octavius in the back of an SUV and told Judge and Batta to stand guard. Then, as I opened the door to the van containing Patch and Nathan, a loud boom sounded behind me, and I felt the ground shake, followed by an intense heat at my back.

I whirled around to see the warehouse in flames and several of my guys, as well as Boar's, on the ground. Fuck! Boar was also sprawled out on his back. I knew that was too easy. I ran back to check on the men. I was relieved to find that no one was seriously injured. It looked to be just a few bumps and bruises.

I extended a hand to Boar and helped him to his feet. He winced in pain and rubbed his chest. "Somebody see if Patch can take a quick look at Boar," I called out to no one in particular.

He waved his hands dismissively. "No need. I'm okay. Just rattled my cage a bit," he said, continuing to rub his chest.

"You sure, man?"

"Yeah. Ain't nothing some whiskey and rest can't fix."

"All right, fuckers, let's get out of here. That fire is going to draw attention, but at least we don't have to worry about evidence. Carbon, you and Shaker toss some fuel on the flames. Wouldn't hurt for it to burn hotter and faster," I ordered.

Shaker nodded looked to Carbon. "Was that climactic enough for you?"

Carbon chuckled. "No, but it'll have to do."

"Well, it sure as fuck was for me. Let's get moving," I barked.

We walked back to our bikes and rode home. I was truly thankful to have rescued Nathan, captured Octavius, and taken care of Annabelle's father with ease. It was rare that any of our missions of that nature were carried out without at least a few people getting hurt.

When I pulled through the gates to the clubhouse, Annabelle was standing outside the front doors waiting for us. As soon as she saw my bike, she ran to me and grabbed my cut right as I came to a stop. "Where is he?" she demanded.

"Relax, doll face. He's in the van with Patch. He's a little banged up, but he's okay," I told her.

"I need to see him," she said, tears running down her face. The doors to the van opened, and Nathan stepped out. "Nathan!" she yelled and took off running. Nathan barely had time to brace himself for the impact. He grunted when she threw herself into his arms.

"It's okay, Mom. I'm okay," he said, trying to soothe her.

"Incoming," Patch shouted from behind Nathan. Nathan looked up in time to see Ember barreling toward him. He lifted one arm and wrapped it around her when she got to him.

"Come on, girls, let's get him inside," I said.

Coal was by the door and held it open for Nathan to enter. "You okay, brother?" he asked.

"I could be better, but I could be worse," Nathan answered honestly.

"Glad they got you back," Coal said quietly.

Nathan clapped him on the shoulder. "Me, too."

When Patch took Nathan to his makeshift med room to finish looking him over, Annabelle turned to me. The concern had vanished from her eyes and was replaced with pure, unadulterated fury. "You," she growled, yes growled, and stabbed her finger in my direction. "You fucking lied to me! You knew what he was capable of and yet you still lied about his death, which not only put me, but my children, in danger! You put my kids' lives in danger, and one of them was nearly taken from me! How could you do that, Phoenix? Did you think it was okay because he's not yours?"

"Everybody, out! Right fucking now!" I bellowed. If we were going to have it out in the common room, we were going to do it without the whole damn club watching, not mention our children and my grandparents who were staring at us with jaws agape.

"Why do you want everyone to leave, Phoenix? So you can feed me some more bullshit behind closed doors? They all knew Octavius was still alive while you made a fool of me. So, let them stay and watch the show. I have nothing to hide."

Holy shit. I had never, and I mean never, seen

her so angry. And I was terrified. Yes, I did lie to her, but it wasn't for the reasons she thought. I needed to speak, but I was too scared to say anything. If I lost her again...Fuck, I couldn't even bring myself to complete the thought.

"Fucking say something, you big bastard," she screamed.

"Mom," Coal said softly. He was standing off to the side with Gram and Pop, but I didn't fail to notice how he was positioned in front of Ember, even though Dash was cradling her against his chest. When my eyes landed on her, I heard her sobs loud and clear. Fuck, this was going to do a number on her, too.

"No," Annabelle fumed. "He's going to explain, and he's got five seconds to start doing it before I walk away from him."

I visibly flinched from the pain that ripped through my chest at hearing her words. I sucked in a huge breath and did the only thing I could. I told her the truth. "We faked his death last year. I wasn't going to let him keep his secrets and spend the rest of his days living comfortably in a jail cell. No, I was keeping him here until he told me what happened to you or I found something that led me to you, whichever came first. When I finally found the papers and headed out to

California, I knew, if I found you, you wouldn't come back here unless he was dead. But what was I supposed to do? I couldn't kill him before I found you!"

"You should have had one of your boys do it before we came back!"

"Fuck, no! If anybody ends him, it's going to be me!"

She stood with her hands balled into fists, glaring at me while she heaved in breath after breath. Then, she shocked the ever-loving shit out of me. "I want to see him."

No. She didn't really ask to see him, did she? "Annabelle, I don't think—"

"I don't care what you think. I want to fucking see him!" she roared. "He ruined my life just as much as he did yours. I have every right to see him and say my piece to him. You owe me that, Phoenix Black."

If I wasn't so busy feeling uncertain and helpless, I might have been turned on by her fierce determination. I swallowed hard and nodded. "Okay. I'll take you to see him."

"Just you. No one else," she added.

Ignoring the shocked and stunned faces in the common room, I silently led her to the cell in the basement where Carbon had secured the little weasel. "Ah, my big bad brother has returned to torture me so soon? I expected it to take you longer to figure things out and clean up the mess you made at the warehouse. Such a messy job disposing of bodies," he taunted.

"I'm not your fucking brother," I growled.

"Our DNA says otherwise," he quipped.

Before I could say anything else, Annabelle shoved me to the side and stepped forward. "Oh, brother dearest, you brought me a surprise. How thoughtful of you to return my lost property."

I growled low in my throat. If Annabelle had something she wanted to say to him, she needed to do it and do it soon, because I was going to snap his neck with my bare hands if he continued trying to goad me.

"I was never yours," Annabelle spat, facing down the man who took so much from her. She stood as tall as she could with her hands clasped tightly behind her back.

Octavius chuckled. "Oh, you still don't know, do you? Well, you would have found out from Nathan at some point, so I'll go ahead and tell you myself. Yes, you were my property. Didn't you think it was strange that I would take in an 18-year-old to provide for while her parents worked off a debt? You were a legal adult. I didn't have to do shit for you. No, your parents didn't owe me any money, and they never worked on the farm. I met your father when I first started providing guns for his club. He was always looking for ways to make more money. He's the one who came up with the idea for loaning money to those who couldn't pay it back and having them work off their debt at the farm. I paid him quarterly for the idea, a sort of royalty, if you will. A few months into it, he asked for his quarterly payment early. He had gotten himself into trouble of some sort. When I refused, he offered you up for sale. So, yes, Annabelle, you are my property."

I had my eyes on Octavius as he spewed his shit at Annabelle. I should have been watching her. If I was, I would have seen her hand move, but I didn't. Before I could react, Annabelle had a gun in her hand and emptied the clip into Octavius without hesitation, not missing a single shot.

We had soundproofed the cell we usually kept Octavius in not long after he became our resident prisoner, but Carbon put him in one of the regular cells until we could get the locks changed on his old cell and there was no way the guys didn't hear the gunshots upstairs. As

I expected, seconds later, I heard the sounds of booted feet running down the hall. The door flew open, and Duke called out as he practically jumped down the stairs with Carbon and the rest of the club on his heels, "Prez! You okay?"

Annabelle whirled around to see a wall of leather with guns drawn and aimed in our direction. She squeaked, and the gun in her hand fell to the floor. "Put the guns down, brothers. We're fine. I need a couple of you to clean—"

I was interrupted by the frantic screaming of my daughter. "Mom! Dad! Let me go before I knock your ass to the ground!"

"Ember! Stop! You know you can't go down there!" Coal yelled back.

"The hell I can't!"

"You two stay up there. We're both fine, and we'll be up in a minute," I called out. "Brothers, give us a minute, yeah?"

Duke glanced around the basement, unable to stop himself from surveying the area for threats. When his eyes landed on Octavius's very dead body and the gun on the floor, he nodded and motioned for the others to go back upstairs. I was proud of him. As my SAA, his job was to protect me at all costs, even if it meant going against my orders.

When I heard the door close, I turned back to Annabelle, who had been surprisingly silent since she fired the first shot. "You okay, doll face?"

She cleared her throat and shifted her weight from foot to foot. "Uh, yeah, I'm fine. So, um, I guess we're even now?"

"Excuse me?"

"You know, you lied to me about him being alive, and I lied to you about wanting to say my piece to him," she sheepishly admitted. When I just looked at her, completely confused, she clarified, "I didn't have anything to say to that bastard. I just wanted to shoot him."

I stared at her blankly for two seconds, absorbing what she'd just said, before I threw my head back and laughed. I pulled her against my chest and engulfed her in a hug. "Woman, I fucking love you."

"Yeah, I love you, too, you big bastard. But let's get one thing straight right now. You ever lie to me again, I don't give a fuck what it's about, I'll superglue your balls to your leg while you're sleeping."

I had no doubt she would. "There is something else I need to tell you. I wasn't intentionally keeping it from you; I just hadn't found a good time to tell you."

"What is it?" she asked.

"Luke called with the results from the DNA sample you provided. It was a match," I said softly, unsure of how she would take the news.

She was silent for a moment and then asked, "What else?"

I cleared my throat. "Your father is also dead. Badger killed him when we went in to get Nathan."

"You're sure he's dead?"

I nodded. "Absolutely. Badger shot him the head. He was dead before his body hit the ground."

She exhaled and her body visibly relaxed. "Remind me to thank him."

I chuckled and threw my arm around her shoulder. "Will do. Let's go see about our kids and let the boys get this place cleaned up."

CHAPTER THIRTY-SEVEN

Phoenix

After reassuring Ember, Coal, and Nathan we were okay, as well as Gram and Pop, I called the officers and Nathan into Church. There were a few loose ends we needed to tie up before we could put this whole mess behind us.

"How did they get you?" I asked Nathan.

"I was driving to the airport this morning, and a truck came out of nowhere. He was all over my bumper and wouldn't go around. I slowed down some thinking he would pass me, but he rammed me instead, which sent me off the road and into a ditch. The next thing I knew, a man was at the window jabbing a needle into my neck. When I woke up, I was tied to a chair in that warehouse," Nathan explained.

"Did they say why they took you?" Badger asked.

"Yeah, they said it was for money. From what I understood, Octavius used to supply guns to the club that Gnaw belonged to. Since the operations at the farm were shut down over a year ago, Gnaw's club has been losing money, or not making as much. Anyway, he said he wanted compensation for some of the money lost. He told Octavius he was going to take Mom, but every time his guy got close to her, one of the Blackwings got in the way."

"Did he say who that guy was?" I asked, trying to contain the rage that was vibrating through my body.

"He said the guy was a prospect for the Disciples of Death. I think he said his name was Kevin."

"What about Crystal, the girl that was in the warehouse? Did they mention how she played into this or what she was doing there?" I asked.

"Yeah, she's Kevin's sister. She was at their clubhouse complaining about Mom stealing you away from her to Kevin. Gnaw overheard their conversation. That's how he knew Mom was back in town. Gnaw tasked Kevin with kidnapping Mom and Kevin got Crystal to help him out. She's the one that told Gnaw about me, and she's the one who took your keys during the wedding reception to let Octavius out," he explained.

"Do you know who shot her and why?" Badger asked.

"She showed up at the warehouse raising hell about them taking me instead of Mom. She was screaming at Gnaw about how he promised to get Mom out of the way so she could have you. She said if they were going back on their word, she was going back on hers and was going to tell you everything. Gnaw shot her in the head before she could say anything else."

I cleared my throat and tried to find the right words. "Nathan, is it going to be a problem for you to keep the events of today to yourself?" I carefully asked. I was hoping he would understand my meaning after having grown up around the Knights of Neptune.

He didn't miss a beat. "Not if you can get your doctor to write me an excuse for my injuries and the drugs that are in my system so that I don't lose my MMA contract," he replied.

I smiled and nodded. "Not a problem. I'll have

Patch take care of that."

"Then I can keep my mouth shut," he said with a grin.

"You know what happened downstairs?" I asked, lowering my voice.

"Nope, not a clue," he said with the corners of his mouth curling up into a mischievous grin.

I chuckled and shook my head. "Go see your mom while we finish up in here. Make sure she's okay for me," I said, though it was more of a plea.

He nodded and rose to his feet. "Will do."

When he left, we immediately discussed how to handle Kevin. He followed my woman, tried to kidnap her, did help kidnap her son, and was instrumental in Octavius's escape. His crimes could not go unpunished. I also wasn't going to let another club make me look like a bitch by letting this go.

I took out my phone and placed a call to the Disciples of Death's president himself. If he knew what one of his members and a prospect were up to or if he planted that whore in my club, he was in for a world of hurt, but I was going to give him the benefit of the doubt. If he didn't know, I was betting he would likely handle Kevin himself.

"Scream," he answered, sounding annoyed

with having to answer the phone.

"Phoenix Black."

"Yeah?" he asked, his tone significantly different.

"Found out one of your members and a prospect of yours were conspiring to kidnap my Old Lady and did kidnap her son this morning. Just got back from handling that actually."

"The fuck you talking about? Which member and prospect?" he barked.

"Member was Gnaw. Prospect is Kevin," I said calmly.

"Motherfucking stupid son of a bitch! Wait, you said 'was.' You killed him?"

"Gnaw, yes. Kevin, no. He wasn't there. His sister was though. Not sure if her whoring for my club was a coincidence or intentional. Doesn't really matter now, I suppose, since she took a bullet to the brain earlier today. What I want to know is if you knew about any of this?"

"Fuck no, I didn't."

"Oh, okay, if you say so then all is well and good," I said, my voice dripping with sarcasm.

"Right. I'll take care of Kevin. Send you proof. Will that do?" he asked. He sounded like he was getting a little nervous, as he should be.

"Possibly. Depends on how you take care of

him and what kind of proof you supply. You have 24 hours," I said and disconnected.

"All right, brothers, we'll see what he comes up with. Good work today. Go enjoy what's left of the day. I believe I have some folks to get to the airport."

CHAPTER THIRTY-EIGHT

Annabelle

Nathan walked out of Church and took a seat beside me on one of the sofas. "How did it go?" I asked.

"It went fine. I answered their questions as best I could and promised not to tell anyone about what happened. That was it," he said.

I huffed. "Well, you're going to tell me about it. What happened?"

"I left for the airport this morning, and some guy ran me off the road. Then, he jammed a needle into my neck. When I woke up, I was tied to a chair in a warehouse with Octavius and another man he called Gnaw. A girl showed up. Then, Phoenix and everybody else showed up.

That's about it, Mom," he explained.

"I'm sorry you had to see him. Did he say anything to you?" I asked, hoping that he didn't say anything that would traumatize Nathan.

"Not really. Just that I was his son and should have grown up under his supervision. He said a lot of nasty things about you. That's when the other man started arguing with him. They had been trying to kidnap you. One wanted to get money out of it while the other wanted to kill you. They were so wrapped up in arguing with each other that they didn't even hear Phoenix and his club come in."

"Do you know who the other man, Gnaw, was?"

Nathan shook his head. "No, just that he was a member of another motorcycle club and that he was looking for you."

I wasn't sure if I should tell him or not. I didn't want to lie to him, but what good would come of him knowing that man was actually his grandfather. On the other hand, if he found out later, he might not be so understanding, particularly since he recently found out about all of the other things I kept from him. Taking a deep breath, I said, "That man was my father, your grandfather."

Nathan leaned back against the sofa. "Ah, that makes more sense."

"What do you mean?"

"Well, they kept arguing about what to do with you once they got you. Octavius kept insisting he got to decide what to do with you because he bought you from the other man years ago."

"Yeah, I just found out about that," I said quietly. "Listen, Nathan, my father was a bad man. I knew that early on in life. Growing up, I never liked my parents, but I never thought my father would sell me. I hope you don't think bad of me, but I'm glad he's dead."

"I am, too, Mom. Anyone who treats you like he did deserves to die."

"Did Phoenix tell you about Octavius?" I asked hesitantly.

"You mean about you shooting him?" he asked bluntly. At my gasp, he continued, "No, he didn't tell me, but it wasn't hard to figure out. The two of you went down to the basement, and then we hear a cacophony of gunshots. Most men don't empty the clip like that, Mom."

I squeezed his arm as one tear slid down my cheek. "I killed your father, Nathan. And I'm in love with your uncle, who is the father of my other children." A sudden realization had me gasping. "Your half-sister and half-brother are also your cousins! Our family is so fucked up."

"Mom, are you serious right now?" Nathan asked incredulously. "First, that man was not my father. Biologically, yes, but not in any other way that counts. Yes, you killed him, but he was going to kill you and I don't believe he would have stopped tormenting us until he was dead. As far as Phoenix being my uncle, it's not like you knew he and Octavius were half-brothers when this whole mess was created. But, if it makes you uncomfortable, I don't have to call him uncle. I'll do whatever makes you happy, Mom. Just know that I don't think any of this is your fault, or Phoenix's for that matter."

My sweet, understanding, mature, wonderful boy. "How'd you get to be so smart?"

He grinned. "I was raised right."

"Nathan, what are you going to tell your team and your coaches?" I asked, suddenly realizing that this situation could have a devastating effect on Nathan's life.

"I already talked to Phoenix about that. He's going to have Patch write me an excuse to cover the bumps and bruises as well as whatever I was injected with. He wants me to stay in Croftridge for a few days to coincide with the story," he explained.

That brought me a tremendous amount of relief. My baby boy had worked so hard to make the team, and his dream was just starting to come true. I couldn't bear it if the ghosts from my past ruined it for him.

Phoenix came out of Church and looked directly at me. "Let's get the kids to the airport."

It took me a moment to realize he meant Ember and Dash. They had canceled their flight earlier when we all learned that Nathan had been taken.

***

Three days later, we were once again driving to the airport, this time to drop Nathan off. Patch spoke with Nathan's coaches and informed them of his car accident and gave them a list of medications administered at the hospital. Luckily, his kidnappers injected him with a very common drug used for sedation.

Once we were on our way back to Croftridge, Phoenix asked, "So, when are you planning on going back?"

I hadn't given any thought to when I would return. Intentionally. I was quite happy living in the moment, and I didn't want to think about reality or the future. That was mainly because I didn't know what to do. I made a home for myself in California. A home for myself and my son. But I had longed for Phoenix for more than half of my life. And I had two other children living in Croftridge. Two children whose lives I had missed most of.

"Uh, I'm not sure. I should probably give Wave a call and see when he's expecting me back," I hedged. Surprisingly, Phoenix let it go.

When we arrived back at his house, Phoenix led me around back instead of going inside. "I thought we could take a walk out to the lake," he explained. He grabbed my hand and pulled me along with him.

I noticed a blanket and a basket on the ground near one of the benches. "What's this?" I asked, gesturing to the basket and the blanket.

Phoenix gave me a Cheshire-like grin. "A picnic. Have a seat."

I sat down and enjoyed a nice picnic lunch with Phoenix. I wasn't sure what it was, but I knew he was up to something. He was far too interested in what I was eating and how much of it I had eaten. He kept pulling things out one at a time instead of laying everything out at once. "Phoenix, what is your deal? You're acting so weird."

He ignored my questions and carried on with his odd behavior. When we were finished, I stood up and dusted my pants off. I turned around and reached for the corner of the blanket to start folding it, and the whole world stopped.

Phoenix was down on one knee, holding a little black box in his hand, gazing at me with so much love in his eyes. "Doll face, I've been waiting 20 years to ask you this question. Will you marry me?"

I couldn't move. I had wanted nothing more when I was 18 years old and, if I was being completely honest, I still wanted nothing more. Were my dreams finally coming true? Was it okay to finally embrace what was right in front of me without worrying that it would be snatched away from me? "Say something, doll face."

I burst into tears and threw myself at him, literally. He caught me with ease and held me tightly. "Yes. Of course, I'll marry you."

Phoenix jumped to his feet. "Good. Up you get. Let's go."

"Wait! What are you talking about?" I asked.

"I ain't waiting around this time. You said yes, so we're going to go down to the courthouse and get married. If you want to do the wedding thing later on, that's fine, but you're marrying me today," he informed me.

"You can't be serious," I said.

"I most certainly am. There's no waiting period in this state. We go down there, get our marriage license, sign it in front of a notary, and turn it back in."

"Wait! I need to talk to Nathan about this. And Wave! What about my job?" I asked. He had lost his damn mind. I couldn't just marry him and hope everything else worked out.

"I talked to Nathan before he left. He said he just wants you to be happy, and if that's marrying me, then he's okay with it." I stood there gaping at him. "As for Wave, I took care of that, too. He said you could work remotely from here, just like you did when you first started working for him. Though I have to say, doll face, you don't have to work. If you want to, that's fine, but you don't have to. Any other protests?"

"I guess not," I mumbled.

"Good. Let's go," he said, taking my hand and speed-walking to his bike.

He drove us into town and parked in front of the only courthouse in Croftridge. We walked inside, filled out the necessary paperwork, and that's how I finally married the love of my life.

EPILOGUE

Annabelle

Three weeks later

I rested my forehead on my arm that was braced on the toilet seat after finishing another round of dry heaving. I wiped away the cold sweat lightly coating my face with my hand and tried to get to my feet.

"It's okay, doll face, I got you." Phoenix carefully lifted me like a child and carried me back to bed. He wiped my sweaty face with a cool washcloth and handed me a cup of water to rinse my mouth.

"I'm sorry," I croaked and started to cry. I don't know why, but I always got teary when I was sick.

"Nothing to be sorry for, doll face," he murmured, smoothing my damp hair away from my face. "This has been going on for several days now, and you're not getting better. Virus or not, I'm calling Patch over to have a look at you." I started to protest, but the look on his face had me clamping my mouth shut.

Patch appeared in our bedroom minutes later. Apparently, he was at the clubhouse and came right over to our house. "Hey, Annabelle. Phoenix tells me you've been sick for a few days. What's going on?"

"It's just a stomach bug. I don't know why he even bothered you. I'm sure it will pass soon," I said.

"I think it would make him feel better if you let me check you over. Won't take but just a few minutes," he replied.

I sighed in exasperation. "Fine."

"Tell me what symptoms you've had."

"I've been throwing up anything I put in my mouth and dry heaving when there's nothing to throw up. I feel weak, and I'm really tired. I've had a few dizzy spells, but no fainting. I've also had some abdominal pain and cramping," I explained.

Patch looked at me thoughtfully. "I see. Any fever?" I shook my head.

He studied me for a moment and sat down on the edge of the bed. "When was your last period?"

"What?" I asked, surprised by his question. "Uh, I'm not sure. I was never very regular after I had Nathan."

"Is it possible that you're pregnant?" he asked.

"No, absolutely not," I insisted. "I had my tubes tied years ago."

He pinned me with a serious look. "Annabelle, tubal ligation is not 100% effective against pregnancy."

"I'm sorry. What did you just say to me?" I screeched.

"I'm saying that there is a small chance you're pregnant. Your symptoms and missing period are prime indicators. Just stay calm. I'll run get a test from the clubhouse, and we'll know for sure in just a few minutes."

I sat there in total disbelief. Why in the hell did I have my tubes tied if it wasn't an effective way to prevent pregnancy? I don't remember them telling me that shit. I thought if you got your tubes tied, you didn't have any more children. End of story.

My disbelief soon turned into panic. I was

too old to have another child. Way too old. Phoenix and I had just gotten married. We were just starting a life together. He knew I had my tubes tied. He wasn't very happy about it at first, but he never mentioned it again. Then, another thought occurred to me. What if Ember got pregnant on her honeymoon? We would be having babies at the same time! Our family was fucked up enough already without adding mother/daughter pregnancies to the mix.

By the time Patch returned, I had worked myself into a complete tizzy. He pulled a box out of his cut and handed it to me. "Here you go. You know how those work, right?"

I rolled my eyes. "Yes, Patch. Pee on stick. Not complicated."

I entered the bathroom, yet again, and stared at the box in my hands. I wasn't pregnant. I had a stomach virus, and I would prove it by peeing on the terrifying little stick in my hand. I took a deep breath and figured it was better to just get it over with. If I didn't do it right then, I would torture myself with the unknown until I was forced to face the situation.

I followed the instructions on the box and placed the stick on the counter when I was finished. Then, I fled the bathroom like I'd found an alien invader in the toilet. I dove into the bed and covered my head with my pillow.

Patch laughed. "I guess that means I have to go get the results."

"You're the damn doctor," I snarked.

Two minutes later, I felt the bed depress from Patch's weight. "Annabelle, you're not sick, sweetheart, you're pregnant."

Phoenix

What in the hell was taking Patch so long? Annabelle swore up and down she had a stomach virus. Patch was a skilled physician. He should be able to confirm that in a matter of minutes. And what the hell did he need to get from the clubhouse? Did she not have a virus? Was it something else? What if she had cancer and they were trying to figure out how to tell me?

Despite my growing panic, I held off a little while longer. When I couldn't take it anymore, I barged into the room, banging the door against the wall. Patch was sitting on the edge of the bed, and Annabelle was sitting up crying. No, not crying, she was sobbing. "What the fuck is going on in here?"

Annabelle raised her reddened eyes to mine

and threw something at me. Not expecting her to hurl an object at me, it hit my chest before I could catch it. I managed to grab the thing before it hit the ground, but it took me a few seconds to realize what I was holding. Then, a few more seconds to read what I was holding. I looked up and met her eyes. "Did you just throw a stick you peed on at me?"

"Is a frog's ass watertight?" she quipped.

I ignored her smartass retort and asked my own question. "You're pregnant?"

She huffed and crossed her arms. "According to that damn stick and this doctor I am. Apparently, tubal ligations aren't completely effective at preventing pregnancy."

Patch added, "She needs to have an ultrasound done to confirm it and make sure it isn't an ectopic pregnancy, which is one that is in the tubes and not the uterus. Ectopic pregnancies are more common after a tubal ligation and are life-threatening. You need to have an ultrasound done sooner rather than later to confirm the pregnancy as well as the location of the embryo."

I smiled, bigger than I think I'd ever smiled before. I strolled over to the bed and pulled Annabelle into my arms. I didn't give a shit what her breath smelled like. She was having my baby, again, and I couldn't have been happier. I captured her lips with mine and let her know just how happy I was.

Patch cleared his throat, reminding me he was in the room. "Sorry, man," I said to him. I redirected my attention to Annabelle. "We'll step out so you can get dressed."

"For what?"

"I'm taking you to have that ultrasound. Patch said the sooner, the better, and I'm not taking any chances with you, so let's go, woman," I ordered.

"Phoenix, I can't just go have an ultrasound. I have to make an appointment first. Hell, I have to find an OB/GYN first," she protested.

"Patch, you can do an ultrasound, right?" I asked.

"Yes, I can."

"Doctor or not, you are not seeing or sticking anything in my hoo-ha!" Annabelle shouted.

I whirled around and looked at her like she had lost her mind. "What are you going on about?"

She rolled her eyes and huffed. "You've probably seen ultrasounds on television where they place the little magic wand on the woman's belly, and it's a wonderful, heartwarming moment. That's not how it happens in the real world. In the real world, they have to shove that magic wand up my hoo-ha and wiggle it around while my feet are up in stirrups to get a good look at what's going on in there. And Patch is not fucking doing it!"

I glared at Patch, and he held his hands up in surrender. "I have a good friend who is an OB/GYN. How about I give her a call and see if she has time to do a quick confirmation ultrasound for you?"

Annabelle huffed. "I guess I could be okay with that, as long as one of you promises to give me something for this relentless nausea."

"If she doesn't prescribe something for you, I will," Patch promised.

Twenty minutes later, we pulled up in front of Patch's friend's office. They were closed for lunch, but she was more than happy to do a favor for Patch. She led us to a room and gave us a few minutes alone so I could undress and get into position. Phoenix stood completely still, taking in everything in the room with wide, almost panicked, eyes while I stripped off my clothes and tried not to puke on him.

The doctor returned a few minutes later, went over my history, explained the procedure, and got started, all the while Phoenix remained in his semi-shocked state. I made a small noise of discomfort when she inserted the wand, and that seemed to snap him out of it. He was at my side in an instant, holding my hand and asking what was wrong.

I was quite uncomfortable, and on the verge of throwing up again, so I snapped, "Let me shove a wand in one of your holes to look around inside your body and see how you feel."

He opened his mouth to say something when the room was filled with a rapid whooshing sound. "That's your baby's heartbeat," the doctor announced. The sound disappeared for a moment when she moved the wand, but it soon filled the room again. "And, that's your other baby's heartbeat. Congratulations! You're having twins."

Phoenix's legs gave out, and he collapsed into a chair that was thankfully behind him while I proceeded to throw up in his lap.

And that was how we found out that we were having twins for the second time.

Also by Teagan Brooks

Blackwings MC
Dash

Duke

Carbon

Shaker

68659060R00196

Made in the USA
Columbia, SC
11 August 2019